"Lucky…

a Bovine Look at
Genius Humanitas

by

Colin Manuel

Illustrations by Shirley Jackson

🍁 PPG

Lucky ... a Bovine Look at Genius Humanitas

E-Book ISBN: 978-0-9918604-3-2
Paperback ISBN: 978-0-9918604-2-5

Additional copies of this book may be ordered by visiting the
PPG Online Bookstore at:

✳**PolishedPublishingGroup**

shop.polishedpublishinggroup.com

or by contacting the author at phone 403-845-4914 or by fax 403-844-8482
or e-mail at colinmanuel@hotmail.com

Due to the dynamic nature of the Internet, any website addresses mentioned within this book may have been changed or discontinued since publication.

Any resemblance between bovine and human characters
and real individuals is purely coincidental.

Dedication

This book is for all those cow-chasers out there.
If ever you have been chased by a cow,
tossed by a cow, loved by a cow,
then this book is for…
YOU!

And to the greatest cow-chaser of them all,
my wife Felicity;
whatever happens,
we did it all together!

Acknowledgement

Crystal Marie Oliver
When Fate led you through that classroom door
all those years ago, who would have guessed
you would become something of a mentor,
a sort of oracle to the north!
Thank you!

Lucky ... Shirley's Illustrations

Table of Contents

Chapter One  In The Beginning

It was all rather dubious, really: I mean my start in life. Okay, the general location was fine. It was a picturesque little farm in the foothills of Alberta with, naturally, a fabulous view of the Rockies—but fabulous only if you go in for fabulous views and that sort of thing. For me, the view of pristine, white snow on a distant mountain peak, set against a backdrop of azure blue, leaves me dead cold. Perhaps that is because it always brings back to me the unfortunate circumstances of my birth—that moment in time when they gave me the name Lucky. The dubious aspects of my arrival were reflected first in my fortuitous purebred parentage, second in the wackiness of my mother, third in the wackiness of the farm proprietorship, and fourth in the wackiness of the weather.

To arrive into a world where it is minus thirty-two degrees Celsius outside, and still dropping, is the epitome of bad timing. My dear mother would have done better to hold her cheeks together, but when the temperature plunged, all her tiny mind could think about was eating. Eating and farting, and emitting that unadulterated and unregulated methane gas so perfect for global warming— something sorely needed at the time, as far as I was concerned. It was as if she had nothing else to do or think about, as if her brain had been shriveled up to the size of a frozen pea by a pressure system over which she had no control. Certainly she never ever gave any thought to her female figure, neither shape nor size, for she always looked as though she was pregnant even when she wasn't. Summer and winter, spring and fall she resembled an untethered Goodyear blimp. Sloppy in her personal habits, she had a tendency to do her personal toiletry wherever she found herself; cleanliness came nowhere near to godliness in her book. Clearly, in her own mind, she had decided that there was no such thing as Nirvana; or perhaps she had resigned herself coming back to this life, after it was over, reincarnated as a dog or a frog. So sloppy was she, in fact, that it took her some time to even register what was happening when and while I was being born, to realize that my birthing was not the mother of all bowel movements but the natural contractions of labour. Even then, she could not, or would not, stop eating. Maybe her subconscious was telling her to fortify herself for another journey into motherhood when the journey had already begun. Who knows?

It was only when her legs actually began to buckle with a major contraction of 6.7 on the Richter scale that she figured it would be better to sit down before she fell down. Then she stretched herself out on her side, right there in slop mostly of her own making, right beside her own high altar, the bale feeder. Let me clarify the picture. My mother was a cow, an old cow—a mature specimen of the genus *Bos*—and I was the ninth in her line of offspring.

Shirley Jackson

Now, being born in slop is one thing; being born in slop in minus-thirty degree weather is altogether something else. Added to this was the indisputable fact that my mother did such an abysmal job of cleaning me off that I was destined for death within less than twenty minutes. Maybe lying there, I was somehow a bit too comatose for her liking; my pathetic efforts at trying to stand on icy birthing fluid had exhausted me much too quickly. Yes, we bovines are classified as outside animals by *Genus Humanitas*—some of my friends would say *Genius Humanitas*— true enough, but then we were never naturally programmed to calve in the depths of winter, either. This is a time when, during the haplessness of birth, you don't have the option of gamboling off into the frost-shine like Daisy the Dancing Dogie in some Disney movie. Moreover, as you feel your newborn body being enveloped by its own dedicated cast of ice there is almost a determination to lie there and wait to be whisked off on the Arctic Express to that bovine playground in the sky. In hindsight, there can be no doubt in my mind that my life on planet Earth would have lasted no more than twenty-two minutes, maximum, had Farmer HWG, Helmut Walter Gronk, not stumbled on the scene, not that his arrival would have necessarily guaranteed my life.

For one thing, Farmer Gronk was none too bright, not a whole lot brighter than many of his cows. That, in and of itself, should not be any condemnation. I mean all of us in this world have to make do with what we are given, even if we are given a little less than we ought to have been given. However, it compelled Herr Helmut to march around with a large, pink cane, a truly unimaginative weapon that he put to rabid use whenever he felt threatened, which was most of the time. To be honest, he would have been better off farming ducks. Heck, he walked like one, so he would have blended in perfectly! Anyhow, as you probably already know, we cows can sense fear, and some of us outright enjoy putting the run on any poor animal that shows it. Helmut's other failing, surely prompted by fear, was to cuss and swear, loudly and with great abandon. Why, that man could cuss the brightest of sunshine into the darkest of darkness and turn the happiest of moments into prolonged periods of pure misery. He must have been awarded a PhD. in cussedness. He must have done extensive and detailed research into all words of four letters beginning with an "F" or an "S". "Gronk by name and gronk by nature" was how old Mabel Threetits described him, and she would know, she had lived on the Gronk spread like forever. We all knew him variously as "Happy Helmut", "Helmut Humpty Dumpty", "Helmut the Haunted", "Walter Gronkite", or plain old "Gronkhead" depending on the severity of any close encounter. Creating additional new names became one of our parlour games.

Now when Helmut got it into his head to barge in on my own private nativity scene, I was quite sure he was the ticket collector for the heaven-bound Arctic Express coming to load me up and take me away. He was quite the sight, more of a spectacle really, something akin to an over-inflated red and yellow beach ball on legs. Elliptical in shape, he was encased in all those things that a cow-chaser might use to make a definitive winter fashion statement. His outer shell was a garish set of red coveralls, undoubtedly stolen from some oil company or other. The reflective stripes thereon gave him an appearance of divine radiance that he had never been known to possess, but at least I was impressed. I was going to be taken away in style!

Helmut took me away all right, with a stream of invective directed at my mother whom he called something akin to "Rewfub", which I discovered later to be a mnemonic for "Red-White-Faced-Bitch" when the name "Rewfub" was fully and properly extended. The invective was, of course, accompanied by a short flurry of beating which did not do a whole lot to endear mother either to Helmut or to me. Worse yet, she almost certainly reasoned that I was somehow the cause of all this inexplicable violence to which she was suddenly and unfairly exposed. So much for the bonding process!

Into the "barn" we went; a totally charitable description for a leaning-into-the-wind clapboard shed with a couple of makeshift pens inside. Riddled with all manner of emergency exits for mice, dogs and cats, skunks and birds, it was as frigid as the weather outside, especially when there was the usual prevailing wind, but at least there was some fresh straw bedding on the ground. Now there's a surprise, my mother followed us in, proving to Helmut that she had at least some interest in my welfare. No doubt she recalled what had happened to former colleagues in the herd when they had played too hard for Happy Helmut to get; they had been consigned to the packers on the "Dog Food Shuttle" within the week. Helmut was not a being blessed with either charity or patience. Indeed, as I have indicated, many of us believed that Helmut was not blessed with much at all. Given his non-aerodynamic profile, the worst thing any cow could do was to make him run. That amounted to a capital offense in his book. My mother's best friend, an old Charolais mama the young-uns used to call Plopsicle, had once made him not only run but fall headlong into a pile of what some say we cows do best. Covered from toque to toe in shades of recycled grassy green, he truly resembled a broccoli soufflé on the march, Mama said. And sure enough, Plopsicle was marched off to the Dog Food Shuttle. Within a day, the big Charolais was gone, never to be seen again, headed off to "Whiskas" glory. But at least her story grew better with every telling.

All of this notwithstanding, that old barn was still a heaven from hell as far as I was concerned. There was the straw bedding and there was the light, not the warming kind like direct sunlight, but light that illuminated things, things that I needed to see. The two small pens were separated by an alley with a homemade head-gate at the end, not that I had any idea what a head-gate might be. All the mothers however, even those who had never been confined in it, saw it as the threat that it was.

"You calves smarten up right now, or I'll get Grumpy Gronk to put you in the head-gate for a day and then you'll listen up to your mother!"

For the uninitiated, the head-gate is simply a variation of the medieval stocks. Farmers would put you in a head-gate if they wanted to beat on you, throw things at you, stab at you with a needle, or fiddle with things that were in need of adjustment or investigation.

But, you guessed it, when it came down to dealing with authority, my mother was an anarchist dedicated to revolution and liberation, to eradicating all exploitation of those who could not speak for themselves. She knew enough not to make Hero Helmut run, but enough to make him work, to keep his feet to the fire, so to speak. She was one of those who could make feigned stupidity into an art form. Cooperation only really occurred when she got tired or when there was a pot of grain at the end of the rainbow. So once we were in the barn, with me in a corner out of the way, Helmut set to work to put my mom into the head-gate. Oh, she was good, so good at not being good; she ran blindly around that pen as if she could not for the life of her see the open alley with its head-gate. Only when The Gronk showed her that there was indeed a pot of grain at the end of the rainbow did she compromise, and this was only after we had endured a torrent of bleep words—enough to make a straight-laced cow's hair curl. The moment she spotted that grain, she was into that head-gate and trapped securely. You could have started sawing her back legs off and she would not have cared in the slightest; she had grain. This was the ultimate bonus, the human equivalent of a banana split with chocolate sprinkles.

Apparently it was now my turn in the spotlight. Helmut hoisted me up in his arms and ferried me over tailside of mom. He lowered me down with more impatience than grace, but at least I could stand on dry ground that didn't resemble an ice rink. I was desperate for victuals, but how was I to know that those great monstrous sausages hanging above my nose were where I was supposed to look? I had enthusiasm, boundless enthusiasm, but absolutely no understanding. Helmut sat himself down on a straw bale, (he was not designed ever to squat), while I set off for an exploration between my mother's front legs, much to Helmut's muttered four-letter-word annoyance. He, bless his granite head, grabbed me by my ears, and while mouthing bleeping somethings about my ancestry he proceeded to force one of the four monstrous sausages into my mouth. So what was I supposed to do with it, chew on it or smoke it? I elected to chew on it.

Mother clearly did not like that for she let loose a kick that thankfully only grazed Helmut's knee as he sat there on his bale. The resultant colourful language seemed to indicate that he was really impressed in some way. At least that was what I was thinking as he proceeded to tie mom's offending leg to a post.

While all of this was going on I didn't see any great need to hang around, so I headed off on my own little voyage of discovery, bleating softly as I went because I felt I had to tell someone how hungry I was. I say bleating because the pathetic noise I was making could hardly have been called mooing. All of a sudden, I found myself hoisted up in the air and back at the buffet. This time an enormous hairy thumb forced my mouth open. Hairy Helmut squeezed some milk down my gullet before shoving the sausage full Monty into my mouth. Oh wow, did that milk ever taste sweet, but where had it come from? Oh wow, this was worth looking for, so I tried a suck. My mouth was filled with bovine nectar. I sucked again. This was terrific; so terrific that I sucked that fat sausage down to the size of a mini-frankfurter. The vibes emanating from Honking Helmut were now more positive, even if he was still calling me something like frothing stupid, or stoopid because it had not occurred to me there were three more sausages there for the taking. He maneuvered another one into my mouth. Again I came to life, my tail taking on a frantic existence all of its own and thumping wildly from side to side. In no time, sausage number two was drained out. Now what? Hey, what's this? Here's another one right alongside, well, what d'ya know? I latched on to it and sucked for dear life, but I was slowing down. My brain was telling me to keep on keeping on, but my belly was telling me that it was about to burst. Still, it was gurgling with definite sounds of contentment, as was good old Happy Helmut.

This was the point at which the other half of the proprietorship walked into my life, the one we all called Gigi. G-G, Governor-General, Gertrude Geranium Gronk was large enough and ornery enough to be a formidable bovine sort of presence all on her own. And that was before she got around to speaking. She had a voice like a rutting Holstein bull; we figured it must have evolved that way after years of trying to communicate with Helmut Hardhat. I should mention here that they say geese and humans mate for life. Deservedly so, is all I can say.

"Oh, that's sure a nice little heifer," Gertie's voice boomed. "Oh I love those colours—that white on her face and them white spots on red. Got to be a throwback to that dumb old Simmental bull we had; you remember, the one you called Ol' Freight Train. Let's call this little beauty Lucky."

Now here was a load of biographical detail I had to absorb in a hurry. So I could ascribe my beauty spots to good Ol' Freight Train of Simmental extraction! Wrong, as I was to find out later. One thing I did know was that any good looks I had did not come directly from my mother, who was, in truth, a purebred Shorthorn that sold below the radar at some auction Helmut had attended. Any beauty she retained was in her genetics, not in the mirror. Better yet, I had started out life with a name, not just a number. There can be no poetry in the number 206, but Lucky? I felt so blessed.

"I brought up the tagger," Gertie Boombox announced next. "Figured you must've found a new critter or something when you didn't come back right away." It sounded more like the bugling of a dinosaur than a message of communication.

"Oh, okay, we'll do 'er now then," his Royal Happiness grunted.

Given all that I had just come through, my next life experience was both traumatic and unfair. Traumatic because there I was—an eighty-pound newborn weakling—suddenly pinned to the ground by a four-ton, asthmatic gorilla. Unfair because how was any life form expected to put up a fight with a being half as big as Alberta lying on top of her? But I was my mother's baby; I did get one kick in at Gertie's knee before I collapsed and surrendered, lying there in the straw awaiting the final *coup de grâce* that I was sure was coming.

"Feisty little bitch, ain't ya?" gurgled Gracious Gertie in her sadistic glory. I discovered that she was as asthmatic as her mate when she bent over me and sent my head spinning with an array of extreme human aromas—dead coffee, stale tobacco, and fermented sweat untamed by any trace of deodorant or oil of coconut. All thoughts of aroma were forgotten, however, the moment that tag was clipped into my ear. I ask you, what species of animal or reptile would want a foreign object like that hanging from the ear for the rest of their days? After all, human beings wouldn't go hanging such things from their lobes, now would they? Like, this thing, this tag, pierced *through* my ear, right through it! I mean, I could not imagine a specimen of *Genus Humanitas* doing such a thing to a fellow specimen. Whoa, hold your horses there, Lucky. What's with that great big brass gong hanging from Gorgeous Gertie's ear? At least my pendant has its own number, 206, just like my mom's. Gertie's has no number and it's big enough for an orangutan to swing from. Hot damn, I'm set for life, eh?

Well, kinda. It was still so bone-chilling cold that I soon forgot about my ear. With my belly comfortably full, all I needed was a place to sleep. Gertrude departed for a coffee while Hardy Helmut now set about releasing my severely irate mama. Having long since vacuumed up the chop in front of her, she had suddenly rediscovered her vocation: mother of a newborn, stalwart protector of her own offspring...all that good stuff. As soon as she was freed, she determined to hasten Helmut's demise or departure, whichever was most practical, and he was made to bolt through the door in a hurry, not that he didn't have something unrepeatable to say about that. No matter, mom was satisfied, triumphant, she had put the representative of all of humanity to flight, and now she had me to herself. She licked me twice and then lay down in the straw beside me, justifiably proud of all her accomplishments.

"That bleeping girl has gotta go this year," I heard Helmut the Heroic yell outside the door. "She's gotten too bleeping big for her boots." I didn't hear the moon's response.

So there you have it, not just the story of my entry into this world but all sorts of useful biographical background in dibs and dabs. Of course, the first thing you will conclude is that the stars were not in the happiest of alignments. The weather was downright mean, and the specimens of *Genius Humanitas* assigned to minister unto my needs were clearly not the pick of the crop. My lineage was apparently linked to some ancient scrub bull with the dubious name of Freight Train, and my mother was halfway between wildly egocentric and borderline psychotic. If I had known then who my father *really* was, perhaps I would have felt much better. See, even Helmut the Honker had not yet figured out that in reality I had been sired by none other than the neighbor's Heartwood's Hero, a purebred Shorthorn bull that had jumped fence and consorted with my willing mother while good Ol' Freight Train was seen heading rapidly for the hills. Shaped too much like his master, he was carrying too much freight to risk a tussle with *Taurus Rex*. The neighbor told Gronky all about that later. Hence my lineage was far more aristocratic than was first thought!

Chapter Two — The Gronk Spread

After that night, I never looked back. We bovines, we're kinda like humans in that respect. Once we've had our fill at the bar, so to speak, we never forget where it is; night or day, rain or shine, like a drunk we can always find our way back. So when Gigi arrived the following morning to check on me, there I was, tail just a-swinging, pulling my breakfast from all four tits. With the amount of milk my mother carried, every meal was a banquet, which is why she had lasted so long in the herd with an erratic temperament like hers. Unfortunately, my success in finding all four tits by myself meant that the Gronks accorded me the Order of the Royal Boot; my mother and I were thrown out of the nice warm barn and herded back into the birthing corral by Gigi herself. That classic old Maurice Chevalier tune came to mind and said it all, you'll know it if you're an oldie, a very oldie, the theme song for the movie *GiGi*.

"Thank heaven, thank heaven for little girls, for without them what would little boys do?"

Er, maybe forget I said this. Gigi wasn't exactly the Gigi of the movie; nowhere near, in fact, and the thought of her doing *anything* romantic with the old Gronk was too much of a stretch for the imagination. See, Gigi had not been a little girl for some fifty years, and with her wheezing along behind us, she wasn't the pretty picture of human femininity that she might have been at seventeen. As for Hairy Helmut, the notion that he could have been a little boy was quite beyond me. And as for a romantic voyage of discovery, let's not even go there! I'm not being uncharitable here—just telling it like it was.

Quite apart from this, going back outside took my breath away. I was quite terrified by all those cows with their big baleful eyes staring at me as if I had just dropped in from some other planet. I need not have worried. Back among her peers, all of my mother's protective instincts came into play. A couple of younger mothers could not resist coming over for a sniff, but mama warned them off with one shake of her head; all but her closest buddy, number 207, a great, big, shambling, camel-like creature with wisps of Longhorn and Chianina, of Brahma and Blonde d'Aquitaine successively showing through, depending on the time of day and the angle of the sun. We all knew her as Rainbow. Anyway, Rainbow ambled over and took it upon herself to tidy up the sloppy cleansing job that Mama had done on me. She had a tongue like a beaver's tail, and about as strong as a beaver's tail if the difficulty I had in staying standing was anything to go by. I looked across at Mama in some alarm. She managed a big yawn, took a mouthful of hay, and then brushed off yet another neighbor showing too much curiosity. Boy, did that tongue-lashing from Rainbow ever feel good! It did not matter that the temperature was still way below twenty degrees Celsius, the blood in my veins was charging off in every direction. Even my ears were tingling. Mama took her time, but she finally came back and took charge, persistently nudging me off in the direction of a calf house in the corner of the corral that was overflowing with bedding. I wandered in to find a few other newborns, not-gonna-move-for-nothing newborns, deep and cozy in the straw. That set the tone for the next day or so, a cycle of filling the belly and then sleeping it off.

Shirley Jackson

Then the weather, or let's say the cold snap, finally broke, and when the sun came out, not only did it shine, it also did in the air what the bedding in the barn had done on the ground. It warmed us through and through. You have to bear in mind that I had never experienced the plus side of Celsius, could never have imagined the incredible sense of well-being that it generated. It was a wake-up call to the instincts; the five calves already born now took off spontaneously and began to race around the corral. Mama, at the bale feeder as ever, cocked her head to check out what was going on and continued eating. But 502's mother, clearly a first-timer, just couldn't deal with it. She came galloping along behind us, bawling pathetically at her offspring who was delightedly and deliberately oblivious to any of her entreaties to stop.

This in turn prompted old 56 to get involved. A huge Ayshire-coloured cow who must have been a real beauty in her day, she was the bovine equivalent of the human "busty beauty", although if any human had been *that* well endowed she would likely have been described as over-inflated or too full of herself. Old 56 was the current granny of the herd; the one who would have worn glasses if she could ever remember where she put them. When she suddenly decided to get into the act, then all forty mamas in the pen, expectant and otherwise, paused in their business to take in the show. Huge tits swaying crazily below the stern, old 56 charged headlong after her bull calf, the one they had named Humpy because all the mamas said he had way too much libido for a young stud his age. Mabel Threetits reckoned he must have had libido even in the womb. Horny Henrietta reckoned he gave new meaning to the designation "pen checker" because he was constantly assessing the possibilities in the playground, when he wasn't playing the fool that is.

People, humans, are sure funny that way. They seem to think only they can possibly possess a sense of humor. How wrong they are in their infinite wisdom. They'd never heard old Mabel Threetits let loose with her rap song "Gonna Have a Farty". In retrospect, maybe that was a good thing. We bovines like a good, regular laugh. We also have our jokers and our clowns. Humpy was the *crème de la crème*. By rights, he should have been a star in Cirque Du Soleil, given his talents. His favourite pastime was to harass poor old Helmut, Ol' Gronkosaurass was what he called him. The one day when His Great Royal Happiness drove into the corral with his big red tractor to drop a bale into the feeder, of course it was Humpy who led the charge straight through the open gate, all nine of us dogies from the corral in tow. Well, they surely could have heard His Royal Wholesomeness in Saskatoon; he was hollering and screeching invective that would have added colour to anyone's world at the same time as trying to exit from his tractor as fast as his bulbous buttocks would allow. Now once again, the hubris of humanity raised its enigmatic head. *Genius Humanitas* is forever ready to congratulate itself for its unrivalled brilliance, and yet *Genius Humanitas* cannot even design a set of steps to allow easy access in and out of a tractor! Happy Helmut did not exactly climb out of his tractor in this emergency; he fell out. Tumbling into nice, warm manure with a sloppy texture is one thing, tumbling head first onto hard, frozen ground is quite another. Poor old Helmut! Although he wasn't knocked out cold, he took his time getting up, too much time in fact, for now three mamas headed out of the open gate for a power walk to someplace else. Another barrage of invective was fired off, volume on full, bazooka shells of expletives and cluster bombs of F-words dropping all around us as Harried Helmut rose unsteadily to his feet. Naturally this was when Humpy and his cohorts came charging back in, minus, you guessed it, the three mamas that had gone off on their own safari, and minus Dough-Head, 72's calf: the same Dough-Head who had contrived to lose the map of his mama's birth canal at birth and had entered this funny old world backwards, which surely accounted for his overall backwardness.

Shirley Jackson

The thing about Humpy is that he was by nature both thick-skinned and boisterous, never a good combination in man or beast. He never even saw Helmut when he charged past the tractor, and flattened him without ever knowing it. Once again, Hapless Helmut found himself stretched full out on the cold, hard ground; all expletives and general other commentary suddenly ceased as he struggled to regain both his breath and his marbles. Fortunately or unfortunately for man, pure unadulterated anger is often a great awakener, arguably one of the most effective transformational forces known to humanity. Happily for Humpy, The Gronk never even saw which animal it was that had laid him so low or else he would have been summarily dispatched by Gronky's coyote rifle in the cab of the tractor. Happily, too, Gigi Gronkette happened upon the scene, and the wayward cows were duly brought back into the corral without undue fuss. Calm is too strong a word, but at least order, or a semblance of it, was restored. Except that Dough-Head had not yet made it back, something his mother was trying desperately to communicate to the man-Gronk who was in no mood to communicate with any body or any thing. Picture it if you can, being a mother to a dopey calf like that; a calf that would never cry out in distress or in an emergency because she would not know an emergency even if she fell into it. Dough-Head was a stargazer, a dandelion-muncher, an ambulatory sniffer of weeds and legumes, a born philosopher of field and pasture. It wasn't old Helmut who figured out what was going on; he was too busy describing what had happened in his version of "A Brief History of Shitty Situations in Short Words." It was Gigi. If Helmut was anything to go by, the male of *Genus Humanitas* is wired for hard rock and machismo; he is a creature who never hears sound variations, and doesn't seem to interpret sound bites very well. So, it was Gigi who realized an hour later that a cow's persistent bawling could only mean one thing; she had lost her calf. Helmut didn't much care; he was just glad to be the right way up.

Humpy was a leader, an incorrigible stirrer of the pot. Two days later when Gronk One delivered another bale, Humpy did it again. He staged an encore performance. With me and several others right behind him, he barreled through that open gate before the Gronk's chubby cheek could detach from its seat. This time though, no cows followed as they were vastly more interested in a fresh green bale. As if to make up for this inexplicable lapse in adult bovine ambition, Humpy led us on an extended circuit with The Gronk hot in pursuit on his two stubby legs, armed as usual with the pink cane and a string of expanded Gronkspeak vocabulary containing terms that nobody should have ever been exposed to. There he was; a complete caricature of himself and yelling something about something and "Get those furry asses ..."

"Just because you humans might be lacking in the furry department ...," I found myself thinking, as I looked at Gronky's bald and toqueless head a second before that pink cane thwacked across my rump, which was as furry as The Gronk said it was.

Pain, sharp and unequivocal, pure pain! I had just been exposed to the most common cattle herding technique used on the Gronk spread. Pain, or the threat thereof, was the classic traffic motivator used by the typical understaffed rancher who does not possess dog or horse. What the dogless, horseless, understaffed rancher always seemed to ignore, however, was how pain could be too often counterproductive. As I was to see time and again, pain often induces anger, and anger begets danger, for human and for animal; it doesn't make much difference. Later on in life, I was to see how one single unrestrained human being armed with a cattle prod could turn a normally docile bull into a murderous killer, but that's another story. As a calf, an adolescent, I was learning the hard way that for there to be order, there had to be discipline.

"Spare the rod and the calf will run wild," is what my mother used to say, almost as if she had betrayed her own kind and gone over to the side of man-Gronk to defend his practices.

Humpy himself was always too smart and too quick to get whacked. He sidestepped the Gronk and ran straight home to mama. We all did then, following our friend, with Gronky thundering along behind us like a giant bowling ball high on Ecstasy. But he had had quite enough of our nonsense. Within a week, he had moved us out of the birthing corral and given us a whole nine-acre field where we could run "all bleeping day if that's what you bleeping-bleepers want." Helmut always made a point of talking to his critters even when he had nothing to say.

Animal husbandry is a complicated business, and every farmer and rancher can make it even more so, as I was about to discover with my second brush with my own mortality. It happened this way. Big 72 calved. In Gronky's eyes, 72 was the best cow in the herd. But her baby was stillborn—never even opened an eye—and no matter how hard she licked that little body, it would not come to life. So the human love affair with numbers, specifically with economics, told the Gronk that he would do well to bring in a foster calf and not waste 72's season. There were no "spare" twins on our place at the time, so Gronky did the unthinkable; he bought a calf at the auction. Now as everybody knows, the thing about an auction is that an animal, especially a very young animal, can be easily exposed to any and all diseases—every virus and bacteria going. It stands to reason with so many animals from different places passing through the premises. The calf that Helmut bought was, ugh, a Holstein steer. Ugh again! It's not that we bovines are racist, but a creature so visually different to us was a natural target. Humpy named the poor wretch Zebroid because of his colouring, and the name stuck for as long as he was around.

Zebroid was very hungry when he arrived. He latched onto 72's tits without ceremony and pigged himself, then pigged down some more. Within twenty-four hours, he had full-blown scours. As fast as he sucked in the milk at the front end, out it came in a recycled and stinky stream at the other. Another twenty-four hours and he was dead: his little body wasted and shrunken with dehydration. But the deed was done. The die was cast, and we all got scours, Humpy, me, all five of us who had been anywhere near Zebroid. Simple, plain old diarrhea is one thing; scours is very much another. You walk around, if you're still strong enough that is, and your sphincter involuntarily lets loose jets of nose-curling, watery fluid. Left untreated, you soon keel over and hang around for the Grim Reaper to come and get you. Humpy and I, wouldn't you know it, were in the worst shape, so the Gronk decided to haul us off to the veterinary clinic in town for treatment. Poor old Humpy couldn't even stand, while I could stay upright for a maximum of twenty seconds before I fell down.

I have to say here, our relationship with the authorities was put on a whole new level now. They went that expensive extra mile for us, picking us up when we were down, and caring for us even when we crapped copiously throughout the back of Gigi's station wagon on the way to town. Helmut was too lazy to hook up his truck to the stock trailer, so his wife's car was left with an odour that could still be detected three years later, no matter how many times Gigi washed it out and regardless how many air purifiers swung from the rearview mirror. Not that we were in any condition to savour our own smell. Mrs. Gigi sat in the back with us, clearly concerned about how her dollars and our lives were about to be expunged.

Shirley Jackson

    The whole thing was a surreal experience for sure. There we were in a clinic where everything was spotless, and we were pooping every which way with absolutely no control. We had two nights on a drip administered by a new breed of humanity we had never before encountered. Whitecoat Smilers is what we called them when they were nice to us, Whitecoat Pricksters whenever they poked something into us. They had this awful habit of smiling benignly at you before sticking a sharp object into your veins, (intravenous), into your muscles, (intramuscular), or under your skin, (subcutaneous). We sort of agreed that this is what we deserved for crapping everywhere (*crappivarious*) and for belonging to whom we did (*Gronkoprecarious*), but they left us with a new regard for some of humanity. Whatever they set about to do on our behalf worked; the gut ache gradually dissipated, the spasms relented, and soon enough we were hollering for our mamas. Truth to tell, like a teenage male, a bovine can take clinical cleanliness for only so long, and neither one of us desired to spend our lives hooked up to a plastic bag dispensing our food from a pole. Give us good old mama tits every time!

We were ferried back home, once again riding in station wagon glory where the odours of our past performance lingered on. Stale in aroma they may have been, but they were ours, all ours, and still a whole lot more nasally palatable than the antiseptic smell of the clinic. Even the Gronks smelled kind of homely. Gigi once again accompanied us in the back to keep us from getting out of a moving taxi.

Oh boy, you should have heard our mamas when they saw us arrive! Both had udders as tight as a drum, both were bellowing their incomprehension at where the hell did we think we had been, and why had we been there. As for us, we couldn't wait to hang off a tit and just guzzle. Even old man Gronk cracked a smile, tempered, of course, by the knowledge that his wallet would be a whole lot lighter. As for Humpy and me, we were inseparable from that day on.

Chapter Three

Pajama Games

What's with *Genius Humanitas* anyway? According to the latest report from "Cowlick Digest" on Moogle, all humans are "manic-obsessive". I can easily see that. Humans are obsessed by economics. Why would so many so-called knowledgeable farmers and ranchers calve out their herds during winter months? Economics. Any fool and his dog can see that bovine survivability would be greatly enhanced if we cows birthed our babies on grass, but no; we wouldn't get big enough and heavy enough for the fall sales when most cattlemen sell off their calf crop by the pound. Economics and numbers, they are what makes the human business world turn. Nothing else matters to them. The more progressive they are, the more they are compelled to play around with numbers. Like a starlet going for a breast implant, bigger and more, that's the meaning of life. It is the "progressives" who implant us with steroids because by the end of summer they want to see us waddling around like "butterball" turkeys ready for market. They weigh us, measure us every which way they can, and then invent yet more ways to tell them things they would do better not to know. They become mesmerized with formulae. They calculate your ADG (Average Daily Gain), your NFE (Net Feed Efficiency), and your EPDs (Expected Progeny Differences). Nowadays, they can even wave a magic wand at the tag in your ear and their computer security blanket will tell them everything about you, when and where you were born, and so forth. Age verification has become a big thing, so they spend all their precious dollars on all sorts of precious technology when all they need do is open your mouth and look at your teeth. Sheesh! Some of them, the more nerdy scientific types, even claim they can calculate how much a cow's fart contributes to global warming! Mind you, if you ever heard my mother farting, you'd not be at all surprised there's a hole in the ozone layer.

"Thank God they haven't yet got around to measuring libido," I used to say to Humpy. "They would put you away as a chronic, repeat sex offender."

What I did not know at the time was that the only reason Humpy remained intact as a bull over the summer was that he was sick, and in the clinic, at the time they would ordinarily have castrated him, converting him into just another run-of-the-mill steer. What I also did not know was that summer was to be the one and only summer we were to be together. I didn't realize in those early days that the basic reason humans kept us around in the first place was to eat us. We were New York steaks on legs, we were mobile filet mignon, ambulatory beef stroganoff and boeuf bourguignon, and we were "real Angus burgers" and "genuine Angus prime rib". We were the best of all red meat, branded as Angus even if we were hang-dog Hereford: succulent and juicy, low in cholesterol, and high in flavour.

Ah, that first summer! Spring was good but summer was awesome. Spring was the harbinger of good things to come; summer was the very essence of good living. Summer was a time when the bumpy road of life was suspended for four months: that bumpy road of vaccination and transportation, of sudden spring snowstorms that froze your bum cheeks together, of cold showers that percolated the cold deep into your body and glued thick mud into your pelt. By summer, though, the frigid temperatures were gone—a distant memory, but a memory, nonetheless, because I lost the tips of both ears as a testament to the frost. Gigi told her mate that I looked like a pixie.

"A lucky pixie," Helmut added, the first time in his life he had veered towards a joke.

At this point, I should tell you about our first encounter with real down-on-the-farm livestock transportation. Our first shitty ride in the back of the Gronk station wagon doesn't count because it was an extraordinary measure. It turned out that we did not get to graze on the home place because there was nowhere near enough pasture, so the enterprising Gronks had rented a three-quarter-section piece of land thirty kilometers to the east, a three-quarter-section that was to be our home for the summer. Now our mamas tried to prepare us for what was coming, but they might as well have been talking of a trip to the moon on Starship Enterprise given the current limits of our life experience. One thing was clear; most every cow we talked to hated the translocation process. Humans have their buses and trains, their ships and their planes; they travel in luxury. What do we have? We have liners and trailers, "pot bellies" and "double deckers". With no luxury whatsoever, who wouldn't just defecate on the floor? Where people riding the subway have something to hang on to if there's no place to sit down, we are simply swallowed up by a cavernous shell of steel. Crammed always to the limit, neighbor crapping indiscriminately on neighbor, we are all squeezed in and the doors are slammed shut. To a calf, the noise is terrifying: the clang of the door shutting and the bawling of stressed-out mamas separated from their babies, all mingled in with the shouts of the people doing the loading.

But I was lucky Lucky, and I had my buddy Humpy by my side. He always looked on such things as a challenge or an adventure, a real blast. I often got to thinking about how he would have made a great human. He was always so full of curiosity and ambition, so versatile and creative; he would have made it to the top of any tree. He would have been the banker with the biggest bonus, the opera star with all the panache of a Luciano Pavarotti, the smooth-talking lawyer who would have used up all of his hot air for a good cause, the builder of his own empire with a vast, gated McMansion to suit. We calves were parted from our mamas in the interests of safety. The mamas were loaded into a cattle liner, but we got to ride in the Gronky stock trailer pulled behind Helmut's wheezy old pickup. Sadly, neither the Gronk nor the Gronkette was into shoveling of any description, so the floor was already knee-deep in stink and ankle-deep in stirred-up manure. Thank the Lord it wasn't a hot day or we would all have choked to death on the fumes. As if our entry into this fetid world was not enough by itself, we started to move. Trying to keep our balance in a moving trailer was a new challenge for us, but then again, we could hardly have fallen down we were so tightly packed in. Still, trying to evade your neighbour's sweet-scented, nervous discharge was well, nigh impossible, so the journey could never be described as pleasant. Just as we had all gotten used to the swaying motion of vehicular travel, we came to a stop.

We heard voices and laughter, we heard door latches sliding, and we all cowered in the front of the trailer, believing that this was it—this was the final step and Judgment Day all rolled into one—all except Humpy who launched into the bovine version of Handel's "Messiah".

"Hallelujah! Hallelujah! Halleluuuuujah!" At least we had arrived at the pearly gates with the appropriate music!

Ah, but it was heaven, a different kind of heaven perhaps. It was a heaven totally unexpected; a heaven of warm sunshine and leafy trees, of delicious green grass, lots of it! Better yet, not even twenty yards away, there were all our mamas streaming off the liner, heads down into fresh green grass the second they hit the ground, munching hungrily on the succulent greenery they had not seen for so long. Oh, how their bags would be full of milk tonight for us babies. Oh there'd be contentment, such great contentment! Humpy's "hallelujahs" only got louder and more boisterous.

Those summer days, especially the first ones, were nothing short of magical: eat, sleep, and romp around with a whole three-quarter section at our disposal. Four hundred and eighty full acres; it was a land as big as China as far as we were concerned. We got to know creatures we had never seen before: the skittish Whitetail doe with her twin fawns, a mama moose that we quickly learned to leave alone in her thicket, the frogs, and the huge barn owl that lived in the giant spruce tree at the corner of what was once a cross-fence. We didn't know, it was not our business to know, that rental pastures such as these represented human victims of their own economics, victims who had bolted or been forced from the business of farming. But then again, talking of minding one's own business, there are those who do, and those who don't. Humpy was one of those that didn't.

One sunny morning found us ambling across the hill, the big hill in front of the farmhouse when he spotted it: a skunk, a big one, that had just exited a long defunct chicken house and was on his leisurely way down towards the river. At least it was leisurely until Humpy got it into his head to challenge this weird-looking creature dressed in Holstein pajamas. Now, the skunk had previously endured close encounters of the bovine kind, and he had discovered that if he held his tail far enough up in the air, most would-be muggers and assassins would quickly get the message and back off. Not Humpy. This was new, this was exciting; this was a challenge he could not let go by, not when all of us other calves were watching him from a safer and more sensible distance. He began dancing and prancing and making fake lunges at this most fascinating of creatures; fascinating, that is, until the precise moment when it did an abrupt about-face and let him have it. Humpy was simultaneously stunned and stinking, not the best of combinations, while the skunk marched imperiously off on his mission. Poor old Humpy! Nobody could stand his presence for about three weeks. And even after that, whenever it rained we were immediately reminded of the incident because the moisture brought out the residual odour from the pores in Humpy's skin. We only saw one other skunk after that, and we gave it a wide berth, letting it go on its way unmolested.

Shirley Jackson

The porcupine, the one we tangled with a month later, was a different story altogether. Once again, the creature was minding its own business doing those things that a porcupine's destiny says it should be doing. But once again, Humpy's curiosity was piqued. After all, this was no skunk in Holstein pajamas; this was a mobile conundrum that needed to be checked out, albeit with more caution than he applied to the skunk. Little did he know he was about to get a repeat lesson of an old axiom, the one that says any animal traversing the landscape before you with the boldest of confidence probably has reason to be so confident and is likely armed with the kind of weaponry that ought not be tested. So what? The animal did not look like a skunk, did not act like a skunk, did not even carry itself like a skunk, and most importantly, did not eyeball him like a skunk. This mobile toothbrush was a whole new phenomenon to Humpy, though what he thought he was going to do with it was anybody's guess. The porcupine was steadfast in its purpose, studiously ignoring the hotheaded adolescent bovine determined to interrupt its innocent intentions. But as it got closer to a huge clump of thick brush, Humpy decided that this most interesting of apparitions was about to be lost to him forever. Foolishly, I followed along right behind him because for me, too, this was not an apparition that should be allowed to go to waste. And then KAPOW, both of us were suddenly running for our lives, both sporting a face full of foreign objects, both wondering what the hell had happened while the indomitable porcupine waddled off on his sober course, unperturbed. With a suit such as his, why would any creature not take him seriously?

Needless to say, suddenly we had to take ourselves very seriously. The spines hung from our muzzles, which swelled up horribly to make the business of suckling from our mothers very difficult, almost impossible. Once again though, I got to believe in my name of Lucky. Even though we had not seen them for over a week, the Gronks came by the very next day with salt and mineral. As we always did when we saw that old red truck appear, we followed it over to the mineral feeder and congregated around, giving Gigi the opportunity to check us over while the Gronk huffed and puffed the bags of mineral supplement into the feeder.

"Oooh nooo!" Gigi howled. "Lucky has had a go-round with a porcupine. Oh oh, number 56's calf has a face full of needles, too."

This was when economics was on our side for once. The moment the Gronks noticed our predicament, it became their predicament because dollar-wise they could not afford to lose us, and we were losing condition fast. The odd spine might fall out by itself, but not all of them. We could easily contract some secondary infection, or, worse yet, die of malnutrition. When economic loss becomes a concern, it's amazing how quick humans will jump into action.

From here on in, the entire exercise was one big pain for all of us bovines, but especially for Humpy and me. For them, the humans that is, this was a porcupine make-work project, something a farmer might go years before having to do. Helmut brought in reinforcements, the neighbor's two teenage boys, each with a fiery red quad that you could hear a half-mile away. We were spooked right from the start, initially by the noise and then by the antics of two crazed youths doing wheelies and doughnuts under the guise of doing a legitimate man's job. Our response was cow-like and simple; in lieu of heading up to the corral a mile away, we headed south toward the muskeg.

Gronky's string of epithets directed at the boys' performance immediately turned into spoken prayer. He was standing in the back of his pickup by now, the four and five-letter words morphing into a long soulful plea: "Please God, don't let 'em get to the muskeg, oh please God, not the muskeg!"

Ah, but these boys were fast. Realizing that they would carry all the blame if the unthinkable happened, they outflanked us and cut us off. Like a herd of caribou in panic on the tundra, we turned en masse and headed east, our eyes now firmly fixed on a heavily treed island in the middle of the pasture. We were the stars of our own movie, "Thundering Hooves, Billowing Dust and Bawling Dogies." And echoing over it all was the Gronk, beseeching God not to let us get into them trees. "Please God, not them trees."

"Why did we bring these buckets of grain?" Gigi had gotten out of the cab and was now asking the obvious question. She was always wary of giving what might sound like too much like advice, especially when her husband was in a state of advanced prayer.

"Uh, grain?" He looked down at the buckets. "Oh yeah, the grain, the bleeping grain, I forgot all about the bleeping grain what with those two bleep-bleep clowns farting about all over the bleeping place. How could I be so bleeping stupid, stoopid?" Gigi could so easily have answered that, but Happy Helmut was just coming to his senses so she knew her timing would not have been appropriate.

Now, as you already know, my good old mama would do just about anything for a mouthful of grain. She was to grain as a Scotsman is to Scotch, as a Cossack is to vodka—you get the picture. So it wasn't the unhired help that saved the day and brought us in, not the quads and the chase, it was the grain. The Gronks, specifically Gigi, drove down to us, with Helmut standing in the back of the pickup. Mama watched him pour a bucket of chop on the tailgate, and Mama was not one to miss out when a treat was on offer. She executed a fancy U-turn and began thundering towards that truck, bringing the whole herd with her. Gigi never got the credit, not that she expected any; she was just glad that potentially she had shortened the day. Mama led the herd straight up into the corral, achieving a number of fair to good licks of grain off the tailgate in the process. For a human to get the idea, imagine a DQ ice cream cone attached to the vehicle in front and you trying to get a lick of it while going full gallop across unfavourable terrain. Helmut was so relieved, and from that day on he ascribed a superior bovine intelligence to Mama when it wasn't intelligence at all; it was the pull of the candy store.

From there, Humpy and I were easily separated from the herd, haltered and tied up to a post whereupon four pairs of pliers went to work to remove no less than sixty-two quills, nineteen from me, the rest from Humpy. We were stoic. We couldn't be anything else when we knew the extreme pain was for our own good. People always knowingly say that animals never really know what's good for them. That's a bunch of rubbish. We knew all right, oh we knew! Nevertheless, if this was high life on the prairies, they could keep it. The pain was excruciating, even if it was so good to be able to suck unimpeded once again. Interestingly enough, too, the incident further endeared us, Humpy and me, to the Gronks. We became their favourites, the ones they first looked for on any subsequent visits. That was to have a pay-off all of its own!

Chapter Four
Head, Heart, Hands & Hooves

Every living creature has to exist in the here and now. The past is history, a collection of memories, both pleasant and unpleasant. The future is the future, unknowable and mostly unpredictable. Unlike humans, most animals do not worry themselves about the past or the future. The present is where it's at; there's no point fretting over what you dimly recollect, no point in second-guessing what the future might or might not hold in store.

So when we made it to that first summer, it was idyllic, as were most subsequent summers, I have to confess. We lived strictly for the moment, never allowing Time and her passage to become enemy or friend. But over time we grew, changed, moving inexorably towards the finality of maturity and the biological responsibilities that went along with it. We did not have the self-imposed responsibilities of humanity; our responsibilities were all in tune with what nature required of us. I was a female of the species, one that caught the eye and held the attention. I was a splendid-looking purebred Shorthorn, well fleshed but not too fleshy. I was straight-backed and held my head high—not as high as an over-strung fullblood mind you, but high enough to be noticed. In short, I was a bit of a bovine prima donna. By the same token, Humpy was morphing into a heavy-set young bull: dark at the neck, nimble on the feet, and spectacular in his colouration. So, in its own way, time was good to us.

The conversation that was to determine our future was actually held back at the home place, over the kitchen table at the Gronk's house. New neighbors had recently moved in on the quarter section adjoining the southern boundary of the Gronk spread: a Mr. and Mrs. Jim and Faith Carberry and their two children: thirteen-year-old Mike, and eleven-year-old Katie, or Kate. For the parents, moving onto their own small farm was a kind of homecoming, for both had grown up on a farm. Jim was now a teacher, and Faith was a nurse, but both wanted their offspring to experience more than the canned and preordained entertainment of the town and the city, more than the instant gratification provided by their favourite TV program.

In short, the parents wanted their children to develop wider connections to the world around them, to the land and to nature. They wanted them to move comfortably in a wider reality than the mall or the Internet and those eternal mind-controlling video games they were drawn to constantly. They needed to experience real life activities like riding a horse, or shooting a deer for the freezer, or fixing a fence, even. Enrolment into 4H was to be a part of the answer: 4H with its structured activities like public speaking and the requirement to raise and sell a calf, 4H with its philosophy of Head, Heart, Hands and Hooves. The kids would learn responsibility and independence and how to project themselves in a formal public setting. At least, that was the goal according to the gospel of the senior Carberrys who themselves had survived 4H, albeit without the distinction they so wanted for their progeny. When Jim was a cool, handsome dude of fifteen years, he had made the mistake of sizing up a potential young female conquest while parading around the show-ring with his calf. The latter, gleefully sensing his handler's inattention, had suddenly bolted for home, flattening a severely overloaded female judge in the process. So overloaded was the judge in fact, that she had to rearrange a couple of critical body parts before she could stand up with dignity, all with a teenage boy and the crowd looking on in awe. Ah, but the kids would never know about that! Although the Carberrys had recently purchased twenty cows of their own, they had no calves; hence, the visit to the Gronks served as both a "howdy neighbor" and maybe a chance to deal on a couple of calves for the kids.

Reserved and perhaps a mite too taciturn, the Gronks had nonetheless always made a point of being good neighbors. They were always ready to lend a hand, as is the nature of a vital rural community. So, when the Carberrys came knocking at their door, cordial greetings were exchanged and the usual pot of fresh coffee was set to brew. After the obligatory discussion of the weather—what it had done and what it was about to do—conversation turned to the generalities of farming, which gave Faith a chance to home in on what they were after.

"Helmet," she said turning on all her prairie rose charm, "Helmet, you don't happen to have a couple of calves we can buy off you, do you? We keep commenting on how nice your cows look when we pass by them on the road. You see, our two children are going to join 4H and they each need a calf."

"Well…." Ordinarily, the "well" would have been a straight up-and-down "no", but the compliment had weakened him, although not yet enough for an outright yes. Anyhow, since he was not a public charity, he wasn't about to give them away, no way!

"Of course we have a couple of calves, HelMUT," interjected Gigi, stressing the correction of her husband's name. "But we will have to have market price for them. You know how it is?" Gigi was never one to shy away from what needed to be said in any business deal.

"Oh, we can do better than that, better than market price I mean," said Faith, determined more than ever that her kids would tread at least some of the same path that their parents had trod before them. While the Gronk was now thinking what an absolute sweetheart the lady was, the son looked decidedly uninterested, while the girl looked, well, indifferent.

"We'll pay you one dollar and twenty-five cents a pound, whatever the weight," said Jim, offering at least ten cents a pound above current market prices.

The Helmet came alive then, almost as if somebody had spilled hot coffee in his lap. Talk of dollars coming his way always gave him a boost, especially if the money was more than he expected. "Sure," he said, one dollar and twenty-five cents a pound will be just fine." The lady could call him "Helmet" any time. "For that price, you can take your pick." He turned to the kids. "You young folks need to come over and pick one out, *jah?*"

"*Jah!*" said Mike, playing the game.

"*Jah!*" said Katie, imitating Mike.

"So you guys come over this time tomorrow, and I'll have 'em all in the corral waiting for you. You know what? You made it just in time. I'm gonna sell 'em all next week—the calves, that is."

The next day, the Carberry family arrived promptly at four-thirty in the afternoon, trailer and all. Gigi was there to meet them, mentally chuckling to herself as the kids dressed in pseudo-western outfits and clearly not liking it one bit, stepped out of the vehicle. No doubt about it, both were feeling horribly self-conscious in their shiny new cowboy boots, the stonewashed jeans and checkered shirts, and, worst of all, the stupid hats. Of course Gigi knew how to pierce through all of this.

"C'mon guys!" she said. Not kids, not cowpokes, not hillbilly wranglers, but just regular working guys. "Let's go up and take a look at them calves. You folks comin'?" She winked at the parents.

"Yeah, we'll tag along," said Jim with a smile on his lips, a grateful smile.

"I want a really, really good calf, a girl calf," Kate pronounced grandly as they set off up to the corral.

"This is so stupid!" Mike was muttering under his breath, furious that he had to leave PacMan for this.

"A girl calf? You mean a heifer?" Gigi pretended not to hear Mike.

"Yes, a girl calf and a really pretty one, one that's nice."

"Oh, I'm sure you'll find one that you want," said Gigi before the parents could intervene and wondering at the same time if this was all going to pan out as they had hoped.

Kids the world over are all the same. They so often hold preconceptions that are wildly off the mark. They may preen and posture and pout about a situation, only to find they had no idea what they were rebelling against. So it was with the Carberry kids. When they got up to the barn, the image of grizzled old Helmut Gronk looking decidedly dour and *very* mean immediately reined in their display of "A for Attitude". And the moment they got involved in the task at hand, why, they forgot all about hostile attitude, western image, and "please-me-now" posture. They were just two kids picking out a pet for themselves, and neither one of them had ever had a pet. As the adults knew they would be, or rather as the adults had hoped, the kids were hooked.

"I like that one, no, *that* one, no that one." Katie was firing off her choices like a politician firing off promises before an election.

"Them ones are all steers," said Helmut a little too gruffly. "The wife said you were lookin' for a heifer."

"What's the difference again?" Kate responded.

"Heifer, girl, steer, boy," said Gigi gently, glad the Carberry parents had remained at the gate. Too many people in the corral could easily spook the whole herd. She noticed Mike concentrating hard, taking note of all that was said. He was way too cool to be asking dumb questions.

"So how do you tell which is which?" Katie persisted, all pretenses at shyness gone.

Mike couldn't resist that one, not with the folks out of earshot. "A boy has a dink, silly."

"Okay, Smarty-pants, that one over there, the one with a white stripe on its face, boy or girl?"

"Boy," said Mike hopefully.

"Girl", said Gigi.

"Boys have a *thingy* under the belly," added Helmut before his wife could continue.

"A *thingy*?" asked Katie.

"A dink, stupid!" said Mike.

Gigi had to rein the kid in. "See the one you were looking at, there's nothing hanging under the belly like that one over there."

It was about this time that "Humpy" and I decided to take an interest in what was happening. "Humpy" had never been bashful about meeting people; he pushed boldly forward to see what was going on, giving Mike a full side view in the process. As usual, I was tagging along behind him when Mike made his announcement. "*Him.* Him. I want him. He's a boy, isn't he? He's got a *thingy* under his belly. A pretty big thingy."

"Ugh," grunted The Gronk. "He's a bull, son, not a steer."

"So now I can't have him? You said…"

"Oh sure, you can have him," said The Gronk, now forced into not calling a spade a "gardening utensil". "You'll just have take his wheels off, that's all."

"His wheels?" This was all becoming a bit much.

"He means his nuts," said Gigi helpfully. "You have to castrate bull calves to make them into steers."

"That's just gross," Katie felt compelled to comment.

"You can pick another one if you want," said Gigi.

"No, I really like him," Mike dug in his heels. "Can you, can you 'er take off his nuts for me?", this addressed to The Gronk.

"I could but I won't," said Helmut. "See, we should'a done him when he was little but we had to leave him because he got pretty darn sick at the time. You'd best get a vet to do it now, he's too big for me. Ain't no big deal for a vet. Won't cost too much either. But as the lady says, you can pick another one."

"No. I want him. He's so cool." And "Humpy" really was so cool at this precise moment. It was almost as if he was on parade for a better life. He was also the biggest calf of the year by far and The Gronk was beginning to see dollar signs tumbling in his mind, seven hundred and fifty times $1.25, now that was better than any cow kick in the ass.

"I want the one next to him," Katie piped up. "The one with the funny ears. Like, it doesn't have a *thingy* under its tummy."

"Oh, oh dear, that's my 'Lucky'. I wasn't going to sell her. I was gonna keep her back as a replacement." Gigi truly did not want to part with me but I went right ahead and sealed the deal so to speak. Kate had walked towards me, her hand extended. I licked her fingers. That was all it took, just a couple of licks, and "Humpy" and I were destined to continue on together. But then again, what did we know? How could we have known that our days of carefree innocence on the Gronk spread were all but over? It was that time of the year when the Gronks would wean and sell their calves to the highest bidder. What had just occurred had simply set the scene for a new chapter in our lives.

"Lucky?" said Kate almost ecstatic. "You actually gave her the name 'Lucky'? I really like that."

"Well, she came so close to dying in the cold when she was born so we gave her the name of 'Lucky'. I can see she really likes you." Clearly Gigi had almost surrendered.

"Please, please let me take her. I'll really look after her, I promise. Mom, Dad, come see my calf, come see 'Lucky'!"

Mrs. Gronk, Gigi, knew then that Katie had taken any decision out of her hands. There was no point in her looking to her Gronk-mate for support, he would be all for taking the money and running. It was too late anyway, both Katie's parents could see the potential of the two animals the children had chosen, and that was before they discovered I was a purebred Shorthorn. What did it matter, they were paying purebred price. They would have preferred Mike to have chosen a female, but they also knew how obstinate their son could be and they did not want to undermine the whole project by forcing him to choose an animal he did not want. That was why they did not protest about taking "Humpy" to the vet to get his "wheels" taken off. As for the Gronks, we represented the first real good money they had made on calves for a good long time. Their world of economics had smiled on them momentarily, momentarily because they knew they should not expect anywhere near the same price for the rest of their calves.

Oh how little did we know! Within the next half-hour, both of us had seen our mamas for the very last time. True, both of them were about fed up with us big hummers hanging off their tits every mealtime. Within those thirty minutes, we had been separated and loaded up into the Carberry stock trailer, just Humpy and me. Now I have to say, that was scary, just the two of us cooped up in this cavernous steel box rattling off into the great unknown.

Looking back on it all later, it seemed as if we landed up in the bridal suite of the Banff Springs Hotel. We shared a freshly bedded pen in a cozy little barn, we were fed a diet of the best hay and grain chop, and we got endless love, human love—hesitant at first but blossoming over time. Of course that didn't stop our bawling for mama most of that first night, and then some more over the next couple of days, but it soon became clear to us that our mamas had fallen off the horizon. We adjusted quickly. How can you not adjust when you have valet service to respond to your every need? There was one bad spell for Humpy—and for me, too, for that matter—when they took him off to town and left me behind. Boy, was I ever panicked, it being the first time I had ever been left in solitary confinement. He reappeared some four hours later, quite stressed out.

"They took 'em," he said. "They took my *cojones*. I'll never be a bull, ever; I'll just be a little choirboy mooing in falsetto." He was pretty distraught, I can tell you, but then so was his buddy Mike and that helped him get over it.

If summer had been idyllic, that fall and winter came close because of all of the attention we received. We became the children's pets; they washed us, groomed us, and taught us to walk like haltered champions.

We loved it, with Humpy always clowning around just enough to let Macho Mike know that he was an eight hundred, eight hundred and fifty, nine hundred pound animal being led by a skinny human being coming in at a scrawny one hundred and fifty pounds. We knew we were being prepared for something big, something momentous, even; a day that when it came was all triumph and tragedy all rolled into one. But again I repeat, what did we know, what could we have known? Every animal is limited by the capacity of its brain, but its existence is defined by its place in the food chain. That is where *Genus Humanitas* scores; a man can and does eat absolutely anything. Look it, the very genius of his brain allows him to eat things that are inconceivable—artichokes and crabs, caviar and sushi—whereas we bovines are stuck with a diet drably vegetarian in its range; legumes, grass, and a little bit of grain. But, fundamentally, we are what we are because of our place in the food chain.

Chapter Five   Hallelujah!

The 4H show and sale was the event that completed the transformation of two self-centered town brats into beings of empathy; people who now recognized that the land was actually out there, people who had begun to see themselves as custodians of all its creatures. We animals are funny. We sensed the excitement building in our human companions, and so we became excited too. The two kids had come a long way, and they had brought us with them. At that show, there was such pride! Oh how proud they were of what they had accomplished, but then so were we. We strutted our stuff for them. We paraded our certain magnificence before the great herd of human folk that came to see us. We positively shone: yet more than this, we were brilliant, and we did it all for them. So for them and for us, the show was a spectacular success. Humpy was crowned Grand Champion. I was Reserve. They hung our winners' ribbons from our halters and paraded us around one more time, and one more again after that for all to see. We had given the kids, the Carberry family, the one-two of victory; we were a *coup*. Ah, but if the show was our very own hubris, the sale was The Great Reckoning—a plunge into a whole new realm of darkness.

Ah, the sale. The word "sale" has its own sense of finality, of transaction completed. I was not entered into the sale because I was destined to be a replacement heifer, due to join the cowherd and to be bred the following summer. Being a steer, Humpy had no such luck. He was to be auctioned off to the highest bidder for slaughter. For sure, Fate had dealt him a great hand thus far, but it was a decidedly short hand. The kids could not help but communicate their sadness, so it was inevitable that we sensed it, that we experienced this heavy sadness for ourselves, and wore it like a funeral shroud. Mike was barely able to hold back the tears as he led his beloved steer back into what was now a sale ring. Completely unfazed by the patter of the auctioneer, by the "Boys, oh boys, would you take a look at those steaks on that critter", Humpy led his handler around that ring with aplomb. As one would have expected from a Grand Champion, he garnered the highest price of the sale, a whopping four dollars a pound, paid by some paunchy oil baron with a flair for bragging rights and a palate for red meat. There was to be no grace period for Humpy; he had been booked into the butcher's for slaughter that very night. Michael Carberry was inconsolable. They had to tear him physically away from a dignified Humpy, and escort him from the building. It was the last time the two Carberry children would enroll in 4H. You can guess how low I felt when Katie led me out to the trailer for the trip home, led me out without my best buddy Humpy. I turned for one last look at the greatest friend I had ever had. He winked and said, "Listen up for me, Luck. I'll be singing 'Hallelujah' in falsetto as I go!" Dear old Humpy, he knew what was coming, and he faced it head on as always.

Shirley Jackson

There is among humanity a school of thought that has never ever considered farm animals as sentient beings. There is a counter school of thought that insists all animals are sentient, have the capacity to emote and feel pain and grief. Oh God, did I ever feel pain, feel grief! A profound loneliness wrapped itself around me and held me captive. What made it undeniably worse was the sad fact that I was still confined to the pen

Humpy and I had shared. I could not help it; I pined for him, ached to hear his foolish moo. Worse yet, the evening after the sale, just on dark, I heard him one last time: not his foolish moo, but a long, soulful "Hallelujah, *Hallelujahhhh…*" Yet, in its way, it wasn't sad but joyous, reiterating for me the notion that whether or not man chooses the time and the place of our dying, we are still likely to be welcomed home by the same creator. I ate little, I sulked, and I found myself utterly indifferent to Katie's love. So they, the Carberrys, made the decision to mix me into the herd, a collection of twenty or so young cows most of which had now calved, it being March.

All of a sudden, I was given something to focus my mind on, "the pecking order" of the herd. As a stranger, an alien in their midst, I was a threat, or something upon which to take out their frustrations. That first day, I had more fights than I'd ever had in my life; not one of them was a play fight, either. But I had been well fed for so long that I was in top physical shape. I had the necessary weight to hold my own, except when two or three cows ganged up on me. Once it became clear to them that I was no pushover, they left me alone, all save this toffee-nosed, purple-blooded Saler purebred that had illusions of being *El Comandante*, Bitch Boss of the Carberry Corral. Oddly enough, the said Carberrys knew that all of this was going on. It was "quite normal," Jim Carberry had to insist to his daughter.

"Well fine," I had to say to myself. Normal or not, if they didn't want to solve the problem, I would, with them looking on. And so it came to pass. Just because she had a bonehead in lieu of horns, she had decided she was the She-Devil in Prada, and it was her mission to put me down. The Carberrys were actually standing at the gate when she made her move. El Bitchoro made a left-flanking maneuver to force me into a corner. I made a quick pirouette, Pierre Trudeau-style, and there she was, right before me in full profile. I charged, a full onslaught with all the cavalry, and banged her straight through the new five-plank fence, slivers of wood breaking off in all directions. Dad Carberry was mad, furious. I had broken his new fence, after all. But LMK, Little Miss Katie, was delighted; her congratulatory squealing immediately spooked the majority of the cows, and some of the calves, out through the hole in the fence and into a field of freshly germinated barley. The girlish whoops of delight quickly faded as the more urgent *basso profundo* of Dad Carberry took over, rendering our stampede for the far corner of the barley field more radical than it needed to be.

It took them an hour, a quad, and a horse to get us all back, and fifteen minutes to patch up the fence with leftover bits and pieces. Was I bothered? Not in the least. My adversary had learned a respect that was renewed constantly over the next couple of months as her two cracked ribs reminded her not to be so inclined to bully. She never threatened me again, nor did any of the others. I became "the Loner", she who preferred her own company or that of LMK. I was that heifer who spent her time dwelling on the memories of the good old days with Humpy. That was, until the day they ushered in Whippet.

We cows are nuts. As you know, when new arrivals come into the herd, the whole herd hierarchy has to be revisited. I kid you not. Some cows have a tendency to indulge in "racial profiling". They're downright racist; there's no other way I can put it nicely. Jim Carberry, Dad Carberry, had purchased a group of five breeding heifers of my age at the auction, or to be more accurate, four breeding heifers and one cast-off; an outcast, the freak that a bidder had removed from the group he was bidding on. So the "freak" was run through the sale ring as a single. The auctioneer was getting exasperated when Faith Carberry came back into the sale hall after getting herself a coffee.

"A quarter, one quarter, boys oh boys, there's nothin' wrong with the animal, a heifer for a quarter a pound, twenty-five cents, how could you ever go wrong…?" Faith's bid was almost involuntary, a quick nod that the seasoned auctioneer was not about to miss. It was the only bid—the bid that turned every head in the place to see who this crazy was—which in turn distracted anyone else from bidding. The auctioneer wanted the animal out, and quickly; he had better things to sell.

"Sold! To…? What's the name, Ma'am?…"

"Faith Carberry. Jim Carberry," Faith shouted. That woke Jim up. Jim who had wanted to bid, but didn't want to appear as if he didn't know what he was doing. Maybe the heifer had a wooden leg, or a glass eye, or something he couldn't see. Not that he would ever confess any of this to his wife.

All eyes followed Faith as she made her way up into the bleachers to sit down in the limited space between her husband and a grizzled veteran of the foothills. The old-timer turned to her and proceeded to make her day. "You know what, lady, you might not know it yet, but you just picked up the deal of the day, let me tell you. There ain't nuthin' wrong with that critter, nuthin' that a few groceries can't fix. She's pretty young, yet, and she's been half-starved, that's all." Faith's quizzical look kept him going. "How do I know? I'm the neighbor of the fellah who sold her. He's run out of money and he's run out of feed. She'll be a darn good cow, you'll see. She's got a bit of Braunvieh in her." At that point, he got up and left, almost as if he didn't want to be caught divulging any more confidential information.

Whippet looked like the whippet she was named after; a racing version of a heifer, streamlined for the prevailing wind, one could say. Charcoal gray, flecked with touches of black and rust, she stood out like a Belted Galloway in a herd of Charolais; the sort of thing that led to a tendency toward racial profiling on the part of humanity and "bovinity" alike. The other four heifers gave her a few shots of their own before she was off-loaded from the trailer, but now her situation was made much worse. There was a wild scrum as various local residents took on the newcomers with great gusto, my old nemesis El Bitchoro trying to stake out Whippet all for herself. As was my habit, I stayed in my neutral corner, chewing the cud and with no intention of fighting anybody who chose not to fight with me. I was a declared pacifist, a peacenik, a conscientious objector, a dove in disguise. That is, until Whippet took refuge behind me, with El Bitchoro pursuing her like an armored carrier at top speed. I saw the hesitation, I watched her veer away with an angry snort, and I knew, I knew then that I was the Empress of my Domain.

Instantly, Whippet and I became the unlikeliest of soul sisters, she with her bulimic physique, and me well-fed and carrying a wide load. I already knew from my days on the Gronk spread that more often than ranchers care to admit, it is the ugliest cow in the herd—the one who looks like an utter weirdo—that invariably raises the best calf, year after year. Humpy's mother, venerable old number 56—with so much tit, so little eyesight, and a hair coat that looked like an old cardigan five times recycled—was a case in point. Yet, as spring wove its way into summer, Whippet put on the pounds. She would always be lean, yes, but she was lean and lithe, and with a bag so perfect she would have been a perfect model for Victoria's Secret.

Ah summer, my second summer: lazy days on fresh green grass, errant grazing in warm sunshine, not a care in the world. Again, it would have been idyllic if it hadn't been for the unwholesome and tiresome business of sex, hormones and sex. Now it is said of the humanity that sex makes their world go round and round; probably up and down, and in and out, if truth be known. A Freudian merry-go-round, their philosophers might insist.

I knew nothing about any of this when the Carberrys delivered the bull into the field. He was a hunk of beef, no doubt about it, and when he immediately set about checking us all out, sniffing at our bits and such, I swear I saw a smile on his face as wide as the garden gate. Thankfully, for me at any rate, both Whippet and I were dismissed in seconds, nothing much to offer Sir Studley Bullshine, I suppose. Sure he was good-looking, if you call a neck like a tree trunk good-looking, and he carried a huge pair of mangoes that hung there as if in their very own shopping bag, but so what, eh? I knew for myself that I did not need him, let alone desire him, but some of the others, why they pestered him shamelessly. But then again, my old mother had never got around to telling me about the birds and the bees, the sires and the studs, and hormones deciding to rage out of control…Well!

There came a day when Whippet abandoned me without a moo of explanation and went traipsing after that bull like some no-good hussy. She was without shame, cavorting about like a stripper on steroids. I simply shook my head in disgust and decided that something more than food might have been missing in her upbringing. She rejoined me a day or so later, grinning like a she-cat and with her tail held straight out as if announcing that she had just had her shot for the glory of the empire. What could I say?

"You're gonna get it too!" She mooed.

Shirley Jackson

"Get what?"

"You're gonna come on heat, whether you like it or not. It happens to all us animals. Even to people. It's called the Rut." I didn't much care for her superior attitude.

"What are you," I asked, "Encyclopedia Mooronica?"

"You'll see," she said a little too prophetically, a sleazy grin across her muzzle.

The first thing I noticed, I couldn't fail to notice, was the sudden interest in my well-being on the part of King Tut himself. Yes, I kid you not King Tut was his name, if you can believe it! To begin with, I simply tried my best to get away from him. But then for some inexplicable reason, courtship suddenly asserted itself, first as a "want", then as a need. An urgent need. An urgent, biological need. Courtship bovine-style is all meat and potatoes. There is no subtlety, no gliding around the ballroom, no Valentine's Day bouquet, no rings on the hoof. It is all strictly biological, an express service with a minimum of style, with foreplay amounting to no more than jockeying for position. It was all so darn crude but apparently effective because I conceived after that first go-round, and that was it. That was sex for the summer, for the whole year! Now I could happily go back to lazy days in the sun, albeit with a swelling belly. Even Whippet whom I had written off as a bit of a trollop, a bit too sluttish for my company, now conducted herself with her former decorum; no more outrageous flirting with the Tut, no more canvassing for you know what.

Once again we spent that summer on rented pasture, this time some thirty miles and a dusty road away from home. But there was a good-sized river running through the pasture, and grass that stayed lush. We prospered, we flourished, and we became a herd that hung together. We romped in that river, we lay in the shade provided by its ribbon of spruce and poplar, and once more we were fooled into thinking those days would last forever. They almost did that year; at least they lasted well into a late fall, but then they came to an abrupt end with the trucking home. We knew now that the snow would not be long in coming. We could feel it, the snow and the cold and the bland diet of dried hay all on the way.

Actually, talking of hay, a subject dear to my vegetarian heart, I have to tell you that hay is as varied as the grass that it's composed of, as varied as the weather in which it was baled. Farmers see some of the differences, but lay folk see none. That particular winter, we had premium hay, nice and green with the aroma of a perfect summer. So we fared well, exceptionally well. But then I have seen subsequent years where Farmer Jim laid out hay that we just stared at, Whippet posing the question on every cow's mind: "What does he want us to do with this, smoke it?"

Winter will never be my favourite season of the year, in part surely because of the traumatic circumstances of my frigid birth. But it does not matter how good the fodder is, there are still days when the cold seeps into the very marrow of your bones where it then takes up residence and hangs around like an unwanted guest. That kind of cold is generally borne on the wind; vindictive and icy, it shows no mercy. *Homo erectus* can, of course, dress up in insulated this and thinsulated that, and yet you will even hear him crying the winter blues. Oh man, many are the times I would have welcomed Fruit-of-the-Loom long-johns for bovines, or even a thick woolen toque to cover my always sensitive pixie ears. As a matter of fact, I think I would look good in a toque—even better in one of those Vancouver Olympic style creations—stuck on the head at a jaunty angle, like some freaked-out snowboarder. We cows are sentient beings, remember, so we too can be fashion-conscious. But I'm wandering because that's all wishful thinking, if truth be recognized. As winter rolled on, I found myself eating more and getting huger by the day, so much so that my dearest Katie began calling me Lucky the Lump. She should have been glad she wasn't eating for two, that's all I can say.

That last month before calving, that is to say the month of February, even running was an activity to be best avoided. I was becoming a couch potato; I even started to look matronly, feel matronly, and felt acutely the something momentous happening inside me. Katie came back into my life as a regular, checking me out every day until that Thursday arrived when she guided me back into the little barn where Humpy and I had spent so much quality time together. It was more of a homecoming than a confinement. Hallelujah! I was so happy not to have to jostle with the others for my food and water, much happier conjuring up those images of Humpy and I in youthful horseplay. Two or three more days passed, and now my bag seemed to have taken on its own life. I felt as if I was about to burst, and so I was, so I was!

Chapter Six

Flights Into The Unknown!

Humankind was given a brain sophisticated enough to allow its people to think at higher levels, although there are times you wouldn't think so when you see some of the shenanigans they get up to. Humans have a habit of getting their noses into absolutely everything, studying this, researching that, exploring the other. Better yet, with their elaborate systems of data preservation and communication, they can pass on their findings and their knowledge. Okay, I admit it, then; when it comes right down to sheer brainpower, we bovines are sadly lacking. A human mother pretty much knows when she is pregnant and about to give birth; even the how and the why are not generally a mystery, even if they might be a regret. So where the human mother is usually informed about her condition, us mama cows have to go through it all on a hoof and a prayer, and with a healthy dose of female intuition. This is quite fine if you are the intuitive type. I'm not. I'm a one-dimensional plodder for whom the whole drama of giving birth for the first time was a protracted trauma, even with a little help from my best friend Katie.

Now, the males of any species prattle on about pain, and pain thresholds, and so forth as if they have always had a monopoly on pain. Even the wimps and the "wusses" among them assume that because of their extreme virility, any pain they experience is somehow more legitimate than that experienced by their female counterparts progressing through the natural birthing process. Ha! They ought to try giving birth just once; that would shut down their nonsense forever!

It was dark outside when my first contraction announced itself, scaring the bejeebers out of me. What had I eaten? What the heck was in the hay? Why was I suddenly heaving like this? I lay down in the straw bedding. Thank heaven the light was on; Katie had left it on deliberately, I guess. What did she know that I didn't know? Another contraction: again, and again and again. I got up to see, to see nothing, to see whatever had all been there before. I lay down. The contractions reasserted themselves, great waves of pain that rippled through my body like a tsunami. What the hell was happening? The door opened and Katie stuck her head in. I got up but was in no mood for huggy-huggies and sweet talk. I was not happy. Kate's gentle tones relaxed me; that is, as far as any creature can be relaxed when her body is trying to conduct its very own symphony in B-major entitled "Bovinius in the Underworld", or some such thing.

"Oh finally, Baby, you're going to have a baby." Katie gushed, oblivious of the inappropriate word repetition. The thing was, she was showing no sign of alarm or panic, no frantic rushing to place a 911 call to the vet clinic, just "Baby, you're going to have a baby." Not that I felt any more informed, but at least if Kate was hanging around then I was surely in good hands. I circled around some more, not for her benefit in particular, but to try and pace things out a little bit. And that was when she spotted the telltale mucous. "Dad says we'll give you an hour or so," she said before ducking back out into the night.

Okay, okay, so there was nothing for it but to lie down, and, in the manner of an outhouse philosopher, to work this thing out. My body was certainly not interested in giving me any choices. The symphony it was conducting was rising and falling to its very own conductor. A couple of times I found my mind wandering to the cows that had calved already, but it never really formed the connection. As far as I could reason, this had to be some new and painful form of constipation. Then on one of the many occasions I was compelled to get up, I smelled the birthing fluid, *my* birthing fluid. Hello, hello, what was all this about now? What was this slimy goop that smelled so familiar, even attractive? It smelled of, well, of me, and I had never smelled so good! All right, for sure I was now embarked on my own voyage of discovery to who knew where. Another hour passed, the contractions grew more regular, stronger, as if I was pushing a giant brick out of my intestines. Kate popped in again, her mom in tow.

"Good girl," Mom said. "The water bag is out. The legs are the right way. See…"

Kate interrupted the impending tutorial. "I hope she has a girl calf, a heifer, because then I'll have two cows of my very own." Once again, there was this human obsession with numbers and accumulation. She made as if to come over and touch me. Mom intervened.

"Leave her be, sweetheart," she said. "You can never be sure how any cow is going to react when she is giving birth; the hormones are all out of whack. We'll come back in half an hour."

The door closed gently, and down into the bedding I went, my body racked with movement: movement of all sorts—foreign movement, movement from inside and outside, movement over which I had absolutely no control. All of a sudden there was one giant spasm, a massive convulsion. That did it. I had had enough. I pushed on that damn rock with all of my strength, felt something give, felt through the waves of pain something very large exiting my body, and I heaved one more time before flopping back into the straw, exhausted. Whatever I had been expelling must have been fully ejected because the spasms now subsided. I lifted my head up to take a look. There, looking right back at me was the biggest pair of unblinking eyes I had ever seen in my life. My heart must have missed a dozen beats at least. What...*what* was it? Was I hallucinating? Had I been eating magic mushrooms? Where on earth had this, this *thing* come from? I was on the verge of outright panic when whatever it was shook its head. My panic was understandably tempered by sheer bloody exhaustion, exhaustion that took hold of my head and flopped it back down in the bedding. But my brain did not, could not stop racing; it was brimming over with apprehensive curiosity. What was it, what was this thing that shook its head at me?

Shirley Jackson

Again I lifted my head, and there they were, two great big, soulful eyes staring straight at me. That was the moment it bawled: a long, plaintive moo calling for attention, love, food, popcorn, and a ticket to the movies—who knew what? But it was enough to kick all of my maternal instincts into high gear. In an instant, I was up on my feet. But what now was all this… this detritus hanging off my rump? The creature mooed a second time. I spun around to face the threat. All it did was blink and shake its head again. For a split second I was totally mesmerized, but something urged me forward to check it out, and the rush of motherhood overwhelmed me. This was mine, this thing, all mine—and I loved it, whatever it was. I began to clean it, lathering it with my tongue, randomly licking ear, head, flank, tail, it did not matter.

The door clicked open and Dad Carberry peered in. "Oh, good girl, Lucky, you've finally done it. Now let me take a look and see what you've got."

That was a big, *big* mistake, and Dad Carberry should have known it. If it had been Kate, I would have had no problem. She was my guardian angel, my mentor, my foot in the human camp. But Dad Carberry, well, while not exactly a stranger, he wasn't exactly my bosom buddy, either. He made his way over to the calf, the calf be darned, over to *my baby*. That was as far as he got. I lowered my head and charged.

Emergency coupled with adrenalin is the finest escape mechanism known to man. Both endow failing older bodies with superhuman qualities. Within a split second, Jim Carberry was up and over the five-foot high plank fence separating my pen from the one adjoining. He would go on to tell an even taller story of how his feet never even touched the ground. That part at least was surely correct; his feet grew sudden wings. But now he couldn't get out of the barn because the exit door from his side of the barn was bolted from the outside. He would have to come back through my pen if he wanted out, and I was having none of it. I had him well and truly cornered. Males of any species are all the same; they hate being held hostage by a female. He was mad. He was fuming at himself because he of all people should have known better, and he was especially mad with me for having taken him by surprise and for putting him to undignified flight. So the next twenty minutes of life passed by rather stressfully for both of us.

Luckily for all though, my attention was suddenly diverted by Tiny, the alien with a mind of his own. Tiny had struggled to his/her/its feet only to tumble back down into the bedding in a jumble of legs and ears. I did some more licking, one eye glued to the activities of the man next door. Again, Tiny floundered up to his feet and began to nuzzle awkwardly between my front legs, wobbling as unsteadily as a Saturday night drunk. This went on for five or so minutes. The alien was clearly looking for something, the pot at the end of the rainbow perhaps, while I myself had not twigged that I was, in fact, the maid from room service designated to deliver Alien's dinner. But then again, it was understandable because I was too preoccupied with the specimen from *Homo sapiens* lurking nearby to be thinking about my duty as a mama to my baby. The outside door opened and Katie looked in.

"Dad, Dad, where are you? Oh Lucky, you've had your baby." Dad was forgotten in an instant as Katie ran over to inspect Tiny.

"Honey, honey, don't go near her! I'm over here. Your dear Lucky put me over the fence."

Too late. Far too late. Katie was already by my side directing Tiny to a tit. I trusted my Katie implicitly. Why wouldn't I? Suddenly I sensed that little calf's mouth close on a tit, felt the hungry suck and the flow of the milk, and a feeling of sheer ecstasy washed over me. I was a mama, just like my mama had been a mama before me. A great pile of afterbirth dropped out of my caboose. I didn't turn a hair; this after all was a new version of heaven.

"You can come out now, but take it nice and easy," Katie directed her father. It was an entirely new experience for him, Mister Macho Cattleman, to be directed and protected by his twelve-year-old daughter. Slowly, gingerly, he scaled that plank fence while I watched with great suspicion, ready to put him right back where he came from. He moved across my pen, and out of the door like a cat on a hot tin roof, and perversely I enjoyed every second of his discomfort. Katie gave me a pat on the rump and departed, closing the door softly behind her. I actually heard her father commence his story. I knew how much it was being embellished by the passion in his voice, but I had no worries. Katie was on my side and Tiny was guzzling like an Irishman hooked up to his Guinness. Oh, I also heard Katie say that Tiny was a girl, and she was going to name her Pucky to rhyme with Lucky. Oh well, these folks had to do whatever turned their cranks I supposed, even if it went as far as bad and sappy rhyming.

Was I a good mother that first year? You bet. Over-protective? Yes. Over-indulgent? Yes. Overly aggressive to anything construed as a threat to my baby? You'd better believe it. Birds, Katie's cat, Katie's dad, the white plastic garbage bag that blew in on the wind, the blue calf sled inadvertently left in my territory, all were given the run. So you can surely picture the brouhaha that occurred when they— the whole Carberry family was on parade for this one—when they decided to tag and vaccinate my baby. Humans pride themselves on being so devious. Even my Katie was in on the conspiracy; she seduced me out of the barn with a pail of chop. I turned just in time to see big brother Mike hustling my Pucky into a corner, but I was too late. The door slammed shut in my face. Okay, at least Katie was with them so they couldn't be doing anything to hurt my baby, or could they? That was the moment when Pucky bawled, a definite cry of pain, a clear appeal for help, an unequivocal message to me that said, "DO SOMETHING!" I head-butted the door. It was solid. I bawled back, I snorted, I stamped my feet like a mad thing. Nothing. I went back to my grain, my mind teeming with evil intentions. I heard the door open and spun around for the final charge of the Heavy Brigade. Pucky was pushed unceremoniously out, and the door closed. My baby stood there, shaking her head vigorously, trying in vain to dislodge a hideous pink tag with the name Pucky written on it in large letters of black ink, as well as the yellow identification button, compulsory for all livestock these days. At first I was nonplussed, but then decidedly angry when I smelled the trace of blood in one ear. I got to thinking darkly about all of the things I could happily hang from a human ear: a cowbell, a three-foot length of chain, a barn utensil such as a shovel or a manure fork. My hate was strongest for Dad Carberry who I believed to be the Big Instigator of All Things Bad. He was, after all the patriarch of the clan: the Grand Initiator of All Things Painful. Would he not look good with a syringe needle pierced through the lobe of his left ear, a metal ring through his bullish nose, or a metal identification tag hanging for life around his neck? I never realized at the time that many specimens of *Genius Humanitas* actually do these things to themselves in the name of self-adornment.

Slowly, over time, I learned to let go. I really had no choice because Pucky herself was such a live wire. She became the ringleader of the Posse, a group of calves so named by the Carberrys for their antics at grain-feeding time. While we moms were chomping down our ration of chop for the day at the feed bunks, the Posse could be seen tearing up and down and around the field, kicking up their heels and enjoying a merry old time. The exuberance of youth is common to all species, I'm thinking, even if humankind would like to claim it exclusively for itself. Always with plenty to eat supplemented by a ready supply of good, clean water, our milk was plentiful and rich that year so our calves flourished. Before long, Pucky had a beam as broad as a fire truck and the weight to match. Only once did she ever slow down; that terrifying once when she somehow picked up a clostridial bacteria from the soil.

Now this was a frightening experience I could have done without. It was I who actually alerted the Carberry Authorities with my frantic mooing. Dad appeared from somewhere to come upon Pucky stretched full out on the ground, frothing at the mouth and kicking at her very bloated belly. He fled, or at least that was what I thought he did, as soon as he saw what was happening. I was convinced, in fact, that he was running from me; the last time I had bawled *in agitato flagrante* at him, I had put him over the fence in a mighty big hurry. I was wrong. He knew what he didn't know and headed into the house to call the vet. Thank God the vet clinic was still open because it was nigh on closing time.

"Try ten ccs of penicillin down the throat, ten ccs of the same penicillin as an intramuscular shot, and get a cup of mineral oil down its gut. If you haven't got mineral oil, use whatever oil you cook with in the kitchen. Do it right now, or the calf will be dead within the hour. If your description of the symptoms is right, she will be back on her feet within half an hour. Sorry I can't do more for you, Jim; I have an emergency caesarian on hand. See you. Best of luck." The phone clicked dead.

Did he have it right? Jim didn't rightly know. He had taken one very quick look at the calf and ran for the phone. He should have checked her out more fully, taken her temperature, checked her pulse, that sort of thing. But he had done none of it, and here he was flying along on a broken wing and a muttered prayer.

At least the kids had gotten home from school. Thank heaven Mike was growing into a solid hunk of a lad. Thank God Kate, my dear, loving Katie, was there to keep things on the right side of heaven, and that Faith, Mom Colonel, was on hand to requisition the needed supplies because Jim realized in one illuminating moment that he had no idea where there was any oil, let alone penicillin. Like a phalanx they approached, with Katie in the vanguard to sweet-talk me out of putting the troops to flight. Mike flopped down over Pucky, not that she was of a mind to go any place, and Dad and Mama Carberry worked together to do their magic. With Faith as a nurse, the injection was not an issue; nor was getting a syringe full of penicillin down Pucky's throat. It was the oil that was the challenge. Faith had actually found some mineral oil as the vet had suggested, but they had to tube it into the calf's stomach. Thick and goopy, it barely moved through the bag and tube designed expressly for fluid ingestion into calves. And Pucky didn't exactly stay still and enjoy it. Eventually though, the job was done. Pucky's first reaction was a burp, the foul smell bringing Mike to his feet in a split second. Kate could not stop me, Dad Carberry could not have stopped me with a two by four, the Pope himself could not have stopped me; I thundered over to check on my baby. She was alive, breathing very raggedly but alive, but why could she not get up?

The Carberrys did the smart thing, the only thing they could do in the circumstances. They retired to the other side of the gate to watch what happened. It was amazing, miraculous. One minute Pucky was lying there completely flaked out, the next minute she had lurched to her feet to stand very unsteadily, as though she was wrestling with the demon drink. Then she hobbled her way to an area of bedding to lie down. The vet was right. Within minutes, she was back on her feet, and within the half-hour, no human would have been able to catch her. It was then that I realized our symbiotic relationship with mankind, and I resolved in my mind that never again would I chase Dad Carberry—well, maybe a little bit to keep him on his toes.

Chapter Seven

Of Teamwork & Separation

My first ever summer on planet Earth in the company of my mother and Humpy had been idyllic. My second summer in the company of Whippet had been equally as idyllic. Well, "idyllicism", (a bovine word invented by a philosophical cow, me), was extended to its outer limits that third summer. We may have been one of the smaller herds in the country, but we had jelled well together, all except El Bitchoro who still retained high hopes of being discovered by a talent scout and offered the lead in a new musical by Andrew Lloyd Webber called "The New Moosical". She was so insufferable that she ended up suffering herself because we excommunicated her. Still, that gave her the opportunity to spend much of her time with the new bull that arrived on the scene, a stud with the oddball name of Hilltop Prairie Invader.

Blessed with a face like that of "Hannibal the Hun", he had the temperament of an alligator with a toothache, but then maybe that was the reason he was so efficient. A heavy-set Red Angus, he wasted no time on the rituals of courtship. To him, mating was clearly like getting on and off a bicycle: mount, pedal like mad, and dismount. That was all there was to it. Then it was back to the shade of the nearest tree to wait for the next item to come up on his agenda. I didn't like anything about him. To me, he was ugly both physically and psychologically, with the bedside manner of a cement mixer. Moreover, being so efficient, he lost very little weight. Having over half a ton of that sort of ugliness covering your haunches in an act of intimacy was like trying to swim the North Saskatchewan River with a fridge on your back. Ah well, at least he was like a well-trained infantryman, swift to the attack, quick to withdraw. Anyway I'm babbling. I never told you about Whippet.

Whippet had given birth soon after me, but her birthing had not been a simple affair. It wasn't her fault; her baby must have been holding the map upside down when he was trying to find his way into the world. He arrived, or rather he endeavored to arrive backwards but one back leg got all hooked up inside. To add to poor old Whippet's misery, her baby was one big boy, a "hummer" Mike called him, with a rump as big as a barrel.

Whippet's timing wasn't that good either, for she contrived to have all her problems at two o'clock in the morning. Once again it was the patriarch of the family, Dad Carberry, who rose to the occasion, literally and figuratively. He usually did a night check of the cows around eleven o'clock, with the first morning check somewhere around five. On this particular day, something woke him and forced him out of bed; good old fart gas from one of Faith's wicked East Indian curries. His tooting was so loud and persistent that he could have passed as the lead trombone in "Farmers' Ragtime Blues". Hell, his sound was positively mellifluous. He decided to go for a walk where any farmer would likely go for a walk at two o'clock in the morning, to check his cows. Why not? It was a beautiful night.

First he decided to look into the barn where he had confined Whippet the previous evening. He opened the door to find her in full *flagrante agitato*, Latin for "very pissed off", because things were not going as they were supposed to. He saw the one leg, *one* leg, one *back* leg, back because it was pointing downwards. His heart sank. Either they all got to work on Whippet in hopes of getting the calf out, or it was a trip to the vet with a subsequent black hole in the wallet. Besides, as always happens in these sorts of circumstances, the truck was not hooked up to the trailer, which in turn was full of square straw bales from last Saturday's auction. He went back into the house to muster the troops. It has to be said that people are far worse than cows when their routines are tampered with, especially if those routines involve sleep patterns.

Faith was up reasonably quickly, but she *had* to have a coffee. Katie was up in an instant and raring to go, while brother Mike heard the call but rolled over and immediately forgot the message. Dad Carberry went back out to the granary to look for a bucket to carry chop in. Ah, once juiced up with the black beverage, there was no stopping *Mon Colonel*, Faith Carberry. Mike was suddenly and rudely reawakened by his mother's emergency screech. There was no ducking this one; it was a call from the Great She Who Must Be Obeyed. A youth awakened prematurely is never a good example of *Genius Humanitas* at its best. With eyes heavy-lidded and barely open; mind coughing up half-articulated questions like, "Wha'? Wha'?", and "have you seen my mumble-jumble?"; feet stabbing aimlessly into a pile of exiled clothing on the floor, in hopes of finding a pair of socks, matched or unmatched; and a hand selecting a pair of jeans that could be allowed to be stained with cow poop, it was a wonder that Mike ever managed to function at all that morning. Katie, impatient with all the foot-dragging, had gone out to "help Dad"—code for "gone to check out the situation for herself." The rearguard, *Mon Colonel* and Private Woozyhead First Class, left the house at 2:30 AM.

Once they got into the barn, it was an entirely different story. Everyone was suddenly very alert, and everyone shared the same vision; they were about to save a life, so they didn't need a mission statement. At least there was no need to explore the problem; it was horribly obvious. Big calf, backwards, one leg folded up somewhere inside. The trouble was Dad Carberry had hands as big as pie plates: great big monstrosities that he could not use effectively to manipulate the calf, no matter how hard he tried. It was to be Mike's coming-of-age.

"Let me try, Dad," he said. What could Dad Carberry do but defer to his son? Faith, looking on, would have loved to have taken over and done her nurse thing, but somehow this had to be Mike's baby.

Mike was (a) strong, now being a fully accredited bale-tossing, shit-shoveling farm boy, and (b) determined. He slid one hand in over the calf's rump, then worked his hand downwards. Even though he found all the blood and the gallons of fluid utterly repulsive, he soldiered on. He got hold of that bent leg and tried to realign it. This prompted a massive contraction; he very nearly yelped in pain as his arm was squeezed as if in a vice.

"Try pushing the calf back in," Katie offered, stating what to her seemed to be the obvious. "Then get his feet together." Dear Katie.

Mike grunted before complying. This was when he felt the calf kick for the very first time.

"It's alive," he said excitedly. "The thing is still alive", he repeated as if to convince himself, if not the others. He pushed the animal back in and reworked the feet so that both were lined up together. Another major contraction, this time with both legs alongside of each other. Faith was there with the calving chains, placing one on each spindly leg, and Jim began pulling. No movement, nothing, the calf was stuck.

"The book says you should pull downwards," Faith pronounced. So Dad Carberry went by the book and pulled downwards. Again, nothing seemed to move. This was when the Head Nurse took charge.

"I'll work the vulva. Mike, you take over one chain; Dad'll pull on the other. Don't pull until I tell you. We have to work with her not against her. Kate, you keep talking to Whippet. Settle her down." All troops had been assigned their duties; it was time for battle to commence.

"Pull," yelled the Commander-in-Chief.

They pulled with little sign of progress.

"Like really *pull* the next time," said Faith. "The book says with a backwards calf you don't have a lot of time because the umbilical cord can break prematurely."

This was an epiphany for Dad Carberry, the realization that he had raised a son who was physically stronger than he was. When Faith had said to really *pull* this time, Mike took her at her word. When the command came again, Mike *really* pulled, and kept the pressure on. Slowly, ever so slowly, the rump started to move. All of a sudden, the calf lay in a twisted goopy pile at their feet…but it was breathing—well, not so much breathing as gasping for air. But that was not enough for the Head Nurse. Faith was bound and determined to use every one of the thirty-one calving tips she had read in *Canadian Cattleman* magazine's "Calving Special".

"Stick a piece of straw up its nostril," she directed Mike. He did. The calf sneezed and its flanks started to rise and fall more steadily. "Blow in his ear," and Mike obliged.

"Let's call him Snippet," said Katie of the right-brain syndrome. "He's so beautiful." Of course she would have been first to note whether the calf was male or female. Whippet was released from the head-gate. This was the moment of truth. Would she accept her baby after all of the distress and the pain, after all the interference she had endured by humans in her private life, or would she decide to have nothing to do with it? This, however, was to be a night of triumph, a story of inspiration. Whippet went straight over to her baby and started cleaning him.

"Time to go, troops," whispered *Mon Colonel*.

Three-thirty or so in the morning is not generally a time of day when humanity excels. But this had been a morning where the lesson learned had been a hands-on exercise about the meaning of life and, in a way, the meaning of death because death had been more of a probability than a possibility. The intense feeling of achievement, of intervening where non-intervention spelled disaster, was a feeling worth savouring. Yes, there was school tomorrow, er today. Yes, the kids would likely fall asleep at their desks, but school was utterly irrelevant in the context of all that they had just learned together. Mike, in particular, had grown exponentially because he had been forced to engage, not forced by anyone but by circumstances, and so he had discovered for himself that there was always a contribution he could make. All he had to do was get involved. It was a lesson that inspired him, stayed with him forever.

Whippet had been fortunate. Had she been purchased by anyone else but the Carberrys at that fateful auction, she would have been recycled into "real beef" cat food. Had she not grown into a sizeable and stylish cow after an early life of poor nourishment, again she would have been a candidate for "Fido's Beef with Gravy". Had she lost her calf at that first birthing, even though it was no fault of her own, economics would have compelled the Carberrys to dump her. You remember how I said humankind is obsessed with numbers? To keep a cow a full year without a calf amounts to a string of zeros. You feed the cow and what do you get: just one big fat zero.

Whippet turned out to be a great mother, caring and attentive and with plenty of milk. So when Mike just had to look in the next morning before going to school, he saw a lively young bull calf skipping around the barn. This pushed Whippet's career into an extended upswing because it was then that Mike decided to buy Whippet in exchange for his farm labour. It was win-win; Dad Carberry did not have to cajole his son into helping out, and Mike got a stake in what the farm produced.

Whippet and I and our babies spent much of that summer sunshine in the glades along the river on the Carberry's rented pasture. It was a dry year so the pasture was not great, but there were all kinds of sweet chews in the riverine brush, all sorts of leaves and berries that we munched on as we explored the treed hillsides where we did not normally venture. It was these extra victuals that pulled us through and gave our babies weights that were not only highly respectable but ended up being comparable to the best weights of previous, greener years.

What I was not to know when we made the trip home from pasture was how far the summer and its warm weather had, in fact, betrayed us. Yields from hay crops were down, way down, and so in the sordid tradition of the numbers game, hay prices only had one way to go: up into the stratosphere. Every farmer and rancher had to take a long hard look at whether to buy hay at such inflated prices or to cull some of their cows. The days of neighbor helping out neighbor were largely over; it was all about numbers and how much profit you could squeeze out of any hay you sold. Humanity likes to pride itself on its humanity, its capacity to look after its own, but where there is profit to be made, the looking after its own went right out of the window. Profit was the new moral imperative. Being relatively new to the ranching game, the Carberrys had no great desire to sell off a part of what they had so painstakingly built up. They opted instead to keep a very tight rein on what was fed and how much. We found ourselves compulsorily enrolled into Weight Watchers that winter, and ended up none the worse for it. But along with all of this, they chose to wean and sell the calves early, in mid-October to be exact, so that we cows could maintain our condition going into winter.

Several of the more tuned-in older cows knew what was coming. Every time it looked as though we might be rounded up for something, they would go into their "hard-to-get" mode and head off into the opposite direction until things quieted down. But the majority of us soon tired of their paranoia and gave up following them wherever they went which is why we were taken by surprise on weaning day when it finally arrived. Oh, how that dreadful day is seared into my memory. Oh, how that day was to rest in infamy, a day of shame and betrayal.

It was the day when two of the family Carberry called us in and served us an unusually generous portion of chop in the small field adjoining the corral. Ah, but it was all smoke and mirrors. Of course we went for it, of course we did; we were hungry. Too late! We looked up to see representatives of *Genus Humanitas* at every gate. On cue, they escorted us into the corral. Pucky and Snippet were still playing hide-and go-seek with each other as we went. The old ones now knew for certain; they had been through all this before. We were escorted into the smaller of two sorting pens, and the sorting began. Calves were held back, and cows were run out. I was panicked, panicked and very confused when they ran me back into the big corral without my Pucky, without my baby who was still of a mind to frolic with "Snippet".

I was crying when the truck came, a huge liner truck that backed up to the loading chute, as it had done on so many farms so many times before. I became frantic when I saw people splitting calves into groups and running them into the truck. The calves were bewildered now, terrified and bawling for mama. Whippet and I both saw Snippet pass by. He didn't even get a last look at his mama before some galoot with a prod urged him forwards, and that was it; he was gone forever. I watched and waited, searched for my Pucky, but she wasn't anywhere to be seen. Where had she got to? She hadn't come by. What had they done with her? What had they done with my baby? I stood there bawling.

"You folks are gonna listen to a bunch of hurtin' music tonight," said a man to Dad Carberry.

"Yep, I guess so," Dad Carberry replied. "Won't take 'em too long to settle down, though, a couple of days or so."

Settle down? A couple of days? What was he on about? And where was Pucky? Where was my baby? The truck came to life with a great roar and began pulling away, the plaintive crying of our babies wafting over to us as they were separated from their mamas forever. It was only then that I noticed a small group of six or so calves cowering in the corner of the sorting pen. O Lord be thanked, I heard her before I saw her, my very own Pucky. I would recognize that call anywhere, even if all I could do was call back. My baby was still here, but why oh why had they separated us? If I had been vain and looked into a full-length mirror, I might have known why at once. I was once more big in calf. I was the picture of a Michelin cow, the blimp that advertises monster tires for monster trucks. I was pregnant big time.

How was I to know Hilltop Prairie Invader had scored an early goal on me, that I was carrying his progeny in my ever-expanding belly? My life to date had only revolved around Pucky, but now an impassable plank fence separated my dear Pucky from me. At least she was there though, alive. Snippet was gone, had disappeared into thin air. As much as Whippet was distraught, there was a component in her thinking that told her how relieved she was not to have her baby's voracious appetite sucking her down every single day. Snippet had been one big boy, and big boys eat lots of groceries. So after a couple of days of pining and crying, she resigned herself to moving on. For me it was much more difficult because Pucky was still around, even if her calling out to me got less and less and then petered out altogether. I still longed for her irreverent company, but an occasional rubbing of the noses through a fence would be all we could manage. She was forced to get on with her life as a replacement heifer. I was forced to get on with mine as a big fat pregnant mama.

Fall, beautiful, golden and short-lived fall, worked its way into the first snow of the so-called winter wonderland. For me, I have to say the only wonder I ever had was wondering when it would ever end. Winter in turn toiled its way through bouts of snow and wind chill fit to freeze any bits of exposed *Genius Humanitas* in seconds, not minutes; that was if any member of *Genius Humanitas* was into exposing his or herself in the first place. We mamas became slow and ponderous, picking our ways carefully on ice-slicked trails to get water from the waterer. Carelessness could lead to a slip, a slip could lead to an abortion, an abortion could lead to a terminal trip on the dog-food truck to the packers. We were a commodity, a consumable—no more, no less.

Chapter Eight

Pick Your Battles!

Ah yes, we are a commodity, that was what I was saying. We wholesale and retail at "x" and "y" cents a pound. As I have said before, we are sirloin and striploin, T-bone and New York, stroganoff and bourguignon. Humans even have posters to show the uninitiated how our bodies are best dissected to arrive at the choicest cuts. Yet even more, we are hides and skins and hooves, we are the source of the dreaded SRMs, Specified Risk Materials, which harbour all those evil prions that gave us BSE.

In all of this then, humanity owes us big time: not the other way round, as some bipeds might claim. Most farmers know and accept this. They work with us day in, day out, through hot and cold and everything in between. They know the happy cow is the productive cow, but now with the overwhelming influence of their economics, there is no room for error and little room for empathy. Cows have to produce and maintain condition, replicate and maintain condition, eat less and maintain condition, and stay healthy, which is of course maintaining condition. The whole story has spawned an industry all by itself. The animal health industry makes millions of dollars in its own right, dollars earned from all the chemicals they stick into us along the way—under the skin and in the muscle, up the nose, and in the ear. Hormones and steroids, antibiotics and probiotics, ultrasound and sounds-around, protein blocks and mineral licks, all engineered for us to deliver bigger numbers. So this led quite naturally to that day in fall or winter that we cows hate, vaccination day and pregnancy-testing day, sometimes combined.

Some cows tolerate handling by humanity reasonably well, while others like me earn themselves a reputation. Given the seemingly natural descent of the Queen's English into "low-flying descriptions" coloured by a certain choice of five and six-letter words, I was routinely called an ornery bitch, a label that didn't exactly jive well with my given name of Lucky. But then again, when it comes down to vaccination and confinement, I was a natural for close-quarter combat, and I was usually ready to play dirty. It seemed eminently fair to me at the time that if some primate of the family *hominidae* gives himself or herself the right to stick a giant needle filled with chemicals into my body wherever it pleases him or her, then I had the right to register my displeasure in whatever way I saw fit. So I became the cow that climbed chute and squeeze, that always turned around in any alleyway designed such that no cow could turn around, that head-butted the Carberry neighbor who had been press-ganged into service without being aware of my criminal record. In fact, it all got so bad that when it came to dealing with me, I was always left to last.

Katie was usually in school on these occasions, so I felt I did not owe loyalty to anybody. You see, we bovines tend to have a limited capacity for loyalty to humans especially when you consider that *genius humanitas* only gets around to handling us when there is some ulterior motive like inflicting pain for gain. Besides, how could I ever bond, coexist, cohabit with a species that took away my Pucky, my friend Katie being the exception. *Homo sapiens* was the prime cause of this uncharitable outlook. And it wasn't as if we had any gospel that told us that we must love our neighbor. My philosophy could have been summed up in one sentence. "We are what we are, so feed us and leave us the hell alone." That was my advice at the time, not that anybody took it or even cared.

So on that vaccination day in December when I was pregnant with my second calf, I staged a command performance. The Carberrys were part of a group of neighbors who came out to help each other on these sorts of occasions, so in addition to the vet, Mork and Anne-Marie were there, and Garth and Marla too, all fortified by yet another East Indian curry lunch put on by Faith Carberry—beef curry, of course. "Eat what you grow" was the Carberry motto. Incidentally, if cows are to be blamed as major contributors to global warming, then those folks who eat curry cannot be far behind. Especially the man they called Mork who was awarded the honorary title of "Doctor Mork" for his efforts to validate the alarming findings of those scientists sounding the "warmist" alarm. Indeed, there was a positive symphony of humanity farting in flats and sharps for the entire afternoon. All of them were seasoned cattle people to be sure, but they were far too much at ease in each other's company for my liking, so there was excessive joking and fooling around. Like, if I'm going to go through intense stress and the people around me are clowning around, naturally I get to figuring that their laughter is at my expense. I resent "absobloodylutely" seeing those who are the prime instigators of all my stress conducting themselves as if they are on the set of Montreal's "Just for Laughs". So right there and right then, I resolved to live up to my reputation; oh, I would give them something to laugh about if that was what they wanted. Or so I thought in my bovine naiveté. My resolution proved to be a mind-altering experience that ensured that never again would I challenge *Genius Humanitas*.

They saved me until the end of the run as they had planned: me and another cow the Carberrys had named Dreadnought because she sported two wicked-looking horns pointing outward like the guns of the famous English battleship. If I had understood the interchange between them, my hopes would have soared. Mork took one look at Dread and me and announced, "I'm done now, I didn't eat enough curry at lunch, so you didn't pay me enough to do these." He started to walk off.

"Wha', what do you mean you're done?" cried Faith, sincerely taken aback. *Mon Colonel* was not happy.

"I mean you didn't feed me enough to cover any more of my valuable time, so I'm going home. C'mon Annie."

"There's beer in the fridge and wine in the cooler," said Faith desperately, even if she was a seasoned campaigner with friends like this.

"Stay put, Annie," Mork directed his wife. Then he turned to Faith, a mischievous grin across his face. "You must have misunderstood me. I said 'we're nearly done'. So bring 'em on."

"Ah, but I'm done," Marla shouted from the back gate, not about to be outshone by such foolishness. "I'm way overworked over here."

Garth looked up from the squeeze. "If you're overworked, then I'm oversexed. How fast can you run?"

"C'mon guys," *Mon Colonel* reasserted her authority. "The wine and the beer are getting too cold." The die was cast; it was our turn to be in the spotlight, Dread first and then me.

The normal procedure was relatively simple. Pack whatever number of animals was in the crowding alley so tightly they had no room to move, then one vaccination into the muscle, another beneath the skin, a dollop of foul-smelling chemical across the length of the back to kill off whatever wildlife was living on us or in us, and step one was completed. Unfortunately, both injections were targeted at the neck, and my neck happens to be very sensitive. Step two required our being moved into the squeeze one cow at a time for the pregnancy test.

Dread was ahead with me pushing behind, thank God; I didn't want *those* horns protruding into my fair buttocks! Jim Carberry (a) knew me well, and (b) retained a memory/grudge forever so had armed himself with an electric prod. It was the only time I ever saw him use one. Naturally, I balked the moment I felt trapped within the confines of the crowding alley, but Jim Carberry knew he had to keep me going forward otherwise I'd be going somewhere else, so he zapped me. Holy cow! A million volt strike of lightning hit me across the rump. Have you ever had a swarm of a trillion bees attack you on the *derrière*? That was what it felt like. I shot forward like the Bullet Train from Paris to Marseilles. The planking along the alleyway gave a sharp crack, but held. A post slid in behind my behind and I was caught. A syringe-wielding hand wavered above me. Ah, but these were hardened veterans, with nobody better than Anne-Marie at administering whatever injection was needed to whatever temperament of cow. She went to pinch the skin on my neck, trying to make the classic "tent" of skin into which to inject the serum. My head went downward and arrived back with an extreme jolt. Ah, but she was a cool dudette, this one; she knew exactly what I was up to and let me shake my head in useless defiance. I paused to see what was happening and in that instant the needle was in and out, subcutaneous shot accomplished. I bellowed anger, I bellowed rebellion, I bellowed Gronkspeak. What I had to say only demonstrated how low I had fallen, for never before had I told humans to combine instant sex with instant travel to get out of my life. The second needle pierced the muscle with a sting like a hornet. Again this prompted another major exhortation to all of humanity to do the sex and travel thing. Even the chemical they poured on my back infuriated me. It stank so bad; it was even worse than that smell of dead soap that most humans wear. Okay, so even if I was playing host to lice and mites and worms and fleas and whatever else, still they had no right to do this to me. Dread was far better behaved. Her problem was her horns. If she, too, resented this gross invasion of her privacy and shook her head to show it, her horns would get caught in the planking. Her obligations completed, she was moved into the squeeze for step two. Quickly tested, she was released just as quickly with a positive call.

Shirley Jackson

My turn. I roared into that squeeze, again like the Bullet Train, and all it did was close on me like a giant set of mandibles. I reared wildly against iron and steel; iron and steel remained immovable. Okay then, if I can't go up, I'll go down. It was premeditated, and so, therefore, it was my own fault. I got stuck. Mightily stuck. I was stuck so badly I could barely breathe. Stuck so badly I risked losing my baby. Sidebars were released, head-gate was released, and still I could not move.

"We won't bother to preg test her," Jim Carberry took control. "We can see the bleep-bleep is pregnant. We just need to get her out." They set to work. They pulled me, pushed me, poked at me, levered me with a couple of posts and a crowbar. Nothing. *Nada. Rien du tout.* Frustrated now and surely thinking about that cold beer in the fridge, Mork grabbed the prod and gave me a jolt. Where the power in my comatose legs came from, I'll never know. I was on my feet in an instant and speeding headlong and henceforth into the sunset.

"Get rid of *her*," said Mork, panting hard: the same Mork who never got rid of a cow in his life, his mantra being "Ugh, she always raises a good calf…"

"Get rid of her," echoed the vet.

"Get rid of that bitch," said Marla, always one to say what was on her mind.

"Me, I would keep her," said Garth. "She's just a tad nervous, like I am when I have to go to the doctor's for a prostate check."

"I can't get rid of her anyway," said Dad Carberry. *"That* is Katie's best friend."

I wouldn't have known what they were saying, that is true, but I did know how utterly traumatized I was. I went and took refuge in the far corner of the field, where we were currently being fed, and shook uncontrollably for at least a half-hour, my heart beating like a tom-tom at an African wedding party. I felt my baby turn and give a kick and I realized two things: (1) he, she, it was okay, and (2) he, she, it was big, very big—much bigger than Pucky had been in the womb. And I came to an inescapable conclusion. I had been vanquished. I concluded that it is far better to fight an occasional winnable battle than to be in a permanent state of undeclared war. From this point on, my attitude changed, my whole demeanor changed. My wisdom had grown exponentially, not my knowledge, mind you, my wisdom. Humankind is too prone to mistake one for the other.

So winter wound its way into the transition between hard winter and soft spring, a time when even the seasons seem schizophrenic or bi-polar, or simply unsure about which side of the sun they should be embracing. My calf was early, too big to remain in hibernation, I guess. He arrived early and he arrived with gusto. Of course it had to be a he—a "hummer", that big. And yes, this time I knew what was happening, but I could never have guessed how quickly it would happen. It turned out that my baby was actually overdue, so the fluid coating most of his body was the colour of rust, a sure sign that he had been hanging around indoors for too long. Once again, I found myself in the barn under my beloved Katie's supervision. It was early evening when she dropped in to check on me, telling me she would come back in about an hour because she had lots of homework to do. So, too, did I. No sooner was she out of the door than the first tremor hit; a big one, at least 7.3 on the Richter scale, and from then on, the contractions never let up. Oh dear, I thought I had discovered pain when I gave birth to Pucky, but this, this was extra-terrestrial. I was stretched to the outer limits of endurance when there was a sudden "WHOMP", and all the pressure was gone. I remained there totally inert. When you give birth to a specimen of your own progeny as big as a shipping container, your body finds muscles it never knew it had, while your regular locomotive muscles simply cannot get it together long enough to get you up on your feet.

In my mind, I went over all of the available information. I had given birth, yes. What I had given birth to was obviously alive because I could hear movement in the straw bedding behind me. But I was also in a state of some shock, not simply my mind and my body, my whole being! I sank into a post-partum trance, my muscles all of a twitch due to the trauma they had just gone through. And suddenly there was dear Kate's face above me, a face furrowed with concern. "Are you okay, Luck?" she said, leaning down and scratching behind my ear. I sat up and from that she knew I was okay.

"Jeez, Luck, old thing, you've just done it, you've just gone and had your baby. That was quick, but how the heck did you ever get it out? It's huge, humongous, and, yuk, it's so gross!" She went over to the calf. "Yep, thought so. It's a boy, a yukky big boy." She came back to me. "C'mon, big girl. It's time to get up and clean your baby." With that she toed me gently on the rump. Not a kick mind you, just a friendly reminder that I had some important business to attend to. I'll say. There seemed to be a lot of blood around this time, which gave me a bit of a scare. Somehow I made it to my feet, and then I saw him and was forced to have a second look—a double take, you might say. He was almost repulsive even to me, his mother, because he was so covered in stale fluid from the womb. But when his big brown eyes blinked at me, all grossness was both forgiven and forgotten. I took a tentative step forward, and down I went like a sack of potatoes. Now Katie was *really* worried. What if I was to fall on top of my baby and crush him?

"Take your time, Luck," she said, again rubbing me behind the ear as she spoke. "Take your time, he'll be fine, he can wait a little. He's one big boy—let me tell you—one very big boy. And you know what his name is, don't you? Yucky. His name is gonna be Yucky because he looks so gross." She talked on at me for a good ten minutes. Finally, I made another major effort to stand. This time I was firmer, stronger on my feet, even if I was still a little wobbly. Within minutes, I was able to shuffle forward and claim my baby, my lucky yucky baby. Katie never left my side. Within the hour, she had seen to it that I had cleaned him off, seen him flounder to his feet and find a tit all by himself. He was one strong baby, and he was not about to be left behind.

Spring, when it came that year, was really spring; not ever too cold, no vicious snowstorms, just leaves popping out on trees, and all of nature focusing on renewal and regeneration. Of course, I gave little thought to anything beyond Yucky and fodder in the feeder, so it came as a pleasant surprise to me the one day to see a group of six near adult bovines, The Group of Six, let into the field to join us mamas. I eyed them suspiciously; they were young heifers, full of themselves, adolescent *prima donnas* who clearly saw themselves as God's gift to the animal kingdom. One in particular—solid red, solid shape—really stood out, a show animal if ever Katie was to need one. I saw her sniff at a cow here, a calf over there, until finally she headed towards Yucky and me. Well, you know me by now: there I was getting all primed up to send her on her way, when something, some instinct held me back. She came right up to me and sniffed, and I sniffed back, and both of us recognized the familiar at the same moment. It was Pucky, my own sweet Pucky. We rubbed noses before she turned to check out my new baby, clearly accepting that she had not been replaced so much as displaced in my affections. As if to show that she understood, she turned and we banged heads playfully, just as we used to do in the old days. For the remainder of that year, we were never far apart, kindred spirits that we were, yet Pucky was smart enough to let me do my own maternal thing, knowing that I had no need of her help.

Shirley Jackson

Ah, that was some summer! Like the spring that preceded it, it was a perfect season. Hilltop Prairie Invader was gone and a new stud took his place, a big Black Angus that some wit had named Beelzebub. We found that name difficult to pronounce so we all called him Bathtub. Happily, Bathtub was slightly more approachable and a veteran of the rut. He did his duty for breed and country, and then like most males he retired to rest. He was like a successful restauranteur; he knew he would get no bonus for multiple servings, nor would he get a mileage cheque for distance covered in the heat of the chase. He did what was required of him then sat in the shade of the nearest tree.

Now it so happened that one of the Group of Six was pregnant, and nobody knew it: not her, not us, and certainly not the Carberry authorities. Hilltop Invader had apparently slipped his gate latch in the fall and got in among the heifers. He was only out seven minutes before discovery, but one minute was all it took. Dad Carberry was around at the time, heard the commotion and herded his bad boy back into his pen, and promptly forgot that anything had ever happened. So this young heifer gave birth entirely unassisted at the edge of a patch of big spruce trees where we liked to lie down. We didn't notice anything, it being around noon, a time when we liked to doze off. Suddenly, there was this calf bawling for help. Well, the place erupted, every mother bawling for her baby and seeking out the problem. And there was the bewildered young heifer on her feet trying desperately to fend off a couple of young coyotes going for her calf. One had a hold of its hind leg, hence the distress call. The other coyote was smart enough to know that it was time to cut his losses and leave, but the first one was too reluctant to abandon such a choice meal. Dreadnought literally speared it with her horn and tossed it away from the calf. Nature angry is nature cruel and unforgiving. We had all felt threatened and we all smelled blood. We trampled that poor coyote into dust. It was brutal, but it was mercifully quick, and the heifer went on to raise her baby. That's how it goes in the animal world. You win some, you lose some, and then there comes the day you lose the big one.

Chapter Nine   *Cool Banana*

That perfect "coyote summer" carried the year in more ways than one. The grazing was good, exceptional, hay yields were excellent, our babies grew to the best weights ever, and we mamas ended up fat, so sleek and glossy we could have posed for the cover of *Cowsmopolitan* magazine, I'm sure. Maybe this was what lulled us into a false sense of security. None of us gave a thought to the weaning day that had to come; I doubt if any of us even remembered the previous year. Of all the cows, I should have been the one to remember because Pucky was there to remind me. But probably because she was still around, my constant companion, I gave it no thought until that awful day when we happened to look up from our "treat" at the grain feeders…and there they were, *Genius Humanitas,* posted at every gate and bolt hole just like last year. Instantly, I knew what was coming. Within minutes we all knew, and within a couple of hours it was all over; we had been robbed of our young, once again. This time though, my baby was gone forever, and I knew it as soon as we were parted. Like before, we were quickly sorted, and like before, the liner came in with a driver much too quick on the draw of the prod. I saw Yucky come by, my big hulking Yucky, and I knew that he knew too. That was it: no ceremony, no sad farewells, a few shouts here and there, the roar of a big diesel engine, and my Yucky was gone, gone as if he had never even existed. Oh how that hurt, really hurt. How painful was the absence of my first ever bull calf, my baby. Yet once the immediate sense of loss was over, profound though it was, Pucky and I were brought even closer, mother and daughter, inseparable friends, and both of us expecting a baby in the spring.

As you can see, the tale of a cow is the tale of the seasons, the story of birth and birth again, of renewal and separation, and, yes, of dying. If we had been left alone in nature, the weaning of our babies would still have happened, but at least the whole business would have been at our discretion and at our leisure, not forced by our human masters. But if we are anything, we cows are stoic; we carry on because we don't have the choice. So in that sense, we are not free enterprisers but citizens of a command economy where all our needs are ostensibly taken care of. We consume and we produce, and as long as that equation stays roughly in balance, we have little to fear. But woe is nigh if we only consume without producing, for then the image of the dog food truck looms high upon the horizon. And frankly, I don't feel comfortable with the image of a Pit Bull named "Freddy" slobbering over my ground beef at the end of my days.

We went through that winter side-by-side, Pucky and me, and Katie too. Let's not forget Katie. In her early days, she may well have been a "town brat", but now she was a farm kid through and through. Actually, nothing slowed either of the Carberry siblings on the farm. Slinging square bales of hay or straw, mucking out the barn, doing the most mundane of chores like feeding the chickens and collecting the eggs, and yes, both of them driving tractor with baler, manure spreader, hay-rake, disc or plow in tow, it all became a part of their vocabulary and who they were. But beyond all of this, they loved their animals. Mike, much more of an entrepreneurial spirit than his sister, had six cows now. Whippet made seven, but he didn't count Whippet because she was special, she was outside of his strictly commercial holdings. Katie had four: Pucky and I, and two other young things, high-stepping Limousin crosses. But we were her pets, the ones she loved to come and pamper or talk to when she was down. We were her confidantes, we knew all about her "boy troubles", about how she really had a crush on this boy Lance who could not even spare even a look her way. Why would he? All the girls were looking at him, the star quarterback of the high school football team. Truth be known, he spent an inordinate amount of time looking at himself. Why not when there was much to see: blue eyes and wavy blond hair and a body to swoon for? Besides, Mommy and Daddy had given him everything he wanted. Why wouldn't they with a son like that?

Katie's crush on the elusive Lance lasted quite some time without ever seeing the light of day. But for some reason, there came a day when she not only attracted his attention, he actually drove her back to the farm in his bright yellow Mustang after a game against the Lindsay Thurber Raiders of Red Deer. Okay, so the roof didn't or wouldn't come down so their hair couldn't stream out behind them, but they could drown themselves in the bass of Dolby surround, a frenetic thumping that obviated any need to talk: a good thing for a very nervous Katie and a lad whose subjects for any conversation were limited in number to the five fingers of one hand. But this was of no concern to Katie because at least she had been *seen* with Lance, and he had let her be *seen* with him, so maybe, just maybe, they would become an item. Maybe, maybe not! It so happened that the day of her first date with Lance was also the day she had put Pucky and me into the barn in the morning because our time was due.

No matter how big his triceps, no matter how magic his throwing arm, Lance was a city boy through and through. Shit on his shoes wasn't an option, a soiled UFA cap on his flaxen locks wasn't cool, and as for gumboots, winter boots, work boots, any boots other than those with cleats, they sent entirely the wrong message. So he refused the loan of boots, headwear and coveralls, of anything that might smell of shit or compromise coolness. Let's face it, such great coolness as he possessed should never be covered up even if he was only going to interview some chick's pet cows with the corny names of Lucky and Pucky. What was this anyhow, "Hillbilly Hollow"?

"Lucky and Pucky, God that's so corny," said Lance, over six feet of languid wisdom. She should have mooned him or marooned him right there, but he was such a looker!

"Come on," she said swallowing the indignities. "You've got to come and see them."

She spotted the slightest of hesitation, glimpsed the momentary flicker of alarm, but failed to read the signs, which he covered up so deftly with coolness. Lance didn't just walk to the barn, he was way too cool to just walk, he sauntered, flexing his throwing arm as he went, and when Katie opened the door, he sashayed right on in behind her without closing the door behind him. I should add here, city folks never make a point of shutting doors or gates because they've never had to worry about what might come in or get out.

Now to most cows, any demonstration of fear is a demonstration of weakness, and weakness in turn is something that very definitely should be exploited, chased, or put to outright flight. We smell fear, sense it immediately, and it unsettles us. We heard Katie greet us, but we could not miss the rising timbre of her companion's voice as he asked, "Er, is it er, is it safe for us to be here?"

His efforts to keep playing it cool caused him to tag along right behind Katie. Well, tag along is perhaps not a good description when the poor lad's instinct for self-preservation had him following so close behind that he bumped into her when she stopped. Katie was Our Beloved, but her suitor was a stranger and we bovines never take kindly to strangers, especially when they are in collision with the objects of our affection. Collision to us appears threatening, and nobody had better dare to threaten Katie when we were around. Even then, the ensuing incident may never have happened if Lance had been watching exactly where on the ground he was putting his high-price Adidas running shoes, white with red racing stripes. Unfortunately, his left foot found a steaming pile of fresh dung deposited by my daughter. He stopped dead and slowly his head tilted to look downwards. Well, you would have thought the world was about to end! The good green stuff had not only covered his Adidas, it was seeping green slop into his Reebok athletic sock. He lost it then and there, lost it completely and began shouting and swearing, using those same four and five-letter words that old Gronky used to use to communicate his displeasure. If Katie was stunned by his outburst, Pucky most certainly was not; she was enervated by it. For a split second she contemplated fight or flight, and chose the latter. Unhappily, Lance was situated between her and a direct line to the open door. Well, she decided on the direct line, notwithstanding, and was gone. Not one to hang around to absorb undeserved abuse by myself, I found myself hot on her heels. Only then did a profound and meaningful silence descend on the barn, and that was when Katie compromised herself and her newfound relationship. How did that happen? How could that be?

Well, there was Cool Banana lying fully stretched out in the straw, face drained of all colour, clothes spattered with many colours, mostly in hues of green and brown. She extended a hand to pull him up. "Are you okay?" she said, clearly very concerned. He dared not answer for fear of bursting into tears. But he did make it to his feet with her help. When Katie saw he was still in one piece, she took a step back and began to laugh. And laugh some more. Every time he tried to speak, she guffawed with laughter. The problem was that laughter was not the most suitable reaction in the circumstances. Like many young hotrods from the sporting world, poor Lance lacked a sense of humor, especially when he himself might be the object of the merriment of others.

"Fuck you and your cows!" he yelled as he made for the door. It was only as he turned to repeat himself that Katie saw the full Technicolour picture. Poor Lance had landed in more than just one cow patty. There was a great gob of the green stuff plastering his flaxen locks to his scalp. There were other gobs of green stuff sticking to other places. Attached to the green stuff were strands of straw from the bedding; this, on a lad for whom clinical cleanliness was next to coolest godliness. No amount of Axe or Sword could have purged that soft aroma of fresh green cow plop, not without a shower first and then a change of clothes. He exited the barn in fury. Katie gave him about twenty seconds to gather himself before she peered out of the barn to see what he was doing. She was compelled immediately to duck back in because she was laughing so hard at the sight that greeted her. Lance was standing by his car. Using his shirt as a sort of carrier bag, he had stripped to his underwear and was busy stuffing all the rest of his clothing into his shirt. With a string of epithets, he threw the bundle into the trunk; there was no way he was going to get cow shit inside his car, no damn way. It was bad enough risking it in the trunk. He even left his prize Adidas behind, and the Reebock socks, they were soiled beyond redemption. He had cloth seats, damn it, and he wasn't about to get any trace of cow poop green on them. So he departed clad only in his underpants, and as one might expect of a young athlete with such great charisma, his underpants left a lot of cheek in the sunshine and boasted a mesh that left little to the imagination.

Ah, but anger can so easily unseat all pretense of rational thought, can push it onto the back burner, can cast it into the realm of sheer "unthinkingness". Stoked up by humiliation and adrenalin, hyped up by the feral throb emanating from his Dolby speakers, Lance's one and only thought was to get home at speed, high speed, as fast as the Mustang would go. Katie heard the rest of the story at school the next day. Never in the annals of true romance had such a beautiful fledgling relationship broken up so quickly and with such a good last laugh.

It was inevitable, really. Lance was so angry, he put the pedal right to the metal and his Mustang responded as it was supposed to. That was all very fine until he got to within five miles of town. Poor Lance was so tied up in his woes, he never even saw the police cruiser come up behind him, all lights blazing. The policewoman, for woman it was, finally had to drive alongside him before getting any kind of response. Lance's reaction was instant and dramatic; he executed the classic emergency stop. The fact that he handled it so well did much to save his bacon; a drunk could never have stopped like that without taking a scenic roll through the ditch. The cruiser pulled up right behind him, its lights still flashing and attracting all sorts of unwanted attention from passing motorists who slowed up as they went by. After all, slowing down when passing a police cruiser with its lights flashing was the law even if the obligatory staring was not. Lance watched the officer via the rearview mirror. She was taking her time, when all he wanted was to get this thing over with. Finally she got out of her vehicle and came over to his window. He let it down. Only then did the rush of incoming cold air remind him of what he was and was not wearing. Instinctively he flushed scarlet and looked down. "Oh my God," was all he could manage as he hunched himself up into a ball, his heart now doing the racing instead of the Mustang's motor.

"Good evening, sir. I'm sure there has to be some reason you were going 165.5 kilometers an hour on a highway posted at 110. Just as I hope there's some logical explanation for you driving around on a chilly night without wearing too much in the way of clothes. Would you care to tell me what's going on?" The ghost of a smile on a not unpleasant face made Lance extremely uncomfortable.

"I, I er, I went to see a girlfriend at er, at her farm and er, and her pet cow knocked me down. I, I er, I was so mad I left in a hurry, and I, I er forgot the speed limit. I know it sounds crazy but it's true, I promise you."

"I see. So this cow, this girl's pet cow, it knocked you down and ran away with your clothes, is that it?" The smile was morphing its way into more of a smirk.

"Yes Ma'am, I mean no, Ma'am. See, I er, I er, I got covered in cow crap, er cow poop, and so I took my clothes off so I didn't get it in my car, the poop I mean."

The officer peered into the car. It was immaculate, the only thing to catch the eye being an empty bottle of Red Bull in the drinks console. Otherwise the car was empty.

"Have you been drinking, sir?" The woman asked the question almost sympathetically, as if she did not want a positive answer. "Or doing any drugs? The more honest you are with me, the easier it will be for you." That's what the cops always say in the movies, Lance was thinking.

"No drinking. No drugs." His reply was not that far above a whisper, it could not have been when all he could do was wonder if and when he was ever going to get out of this nightmare. The officer's answer only made it worse, far worse.

"Would you please step outside of your car for a minute while I check it out?"

"Ugh, Ma'am, do I really have to?" Not the best question to ask a fully clothed custodian of the law who was starting to get cold from standing outside so long.

"Yes, I'm afraid you will have to. Thirty seconds is all it will take."

Slowly, reluctantly, Lance uncurled himself and stepped outside of his car while the officer jumped in to check it out more fully. Nothing but the empty bottle of Red Bull. "That's appropriate," she said to herself as she got out.

"So where are your clothes?" she asked.

"Oh, oh," he stuttered before saying what he should have reemphasized right at the beginning, "my clothes are in the trunk."

"Then pop the trunk and show me."

He did so, and while she carried out her inspection, he was left standing there to freeze, clad only in a pair of lime green underpants—not boxer shorts, not Stanfield winter woolens, but a low-slung net creation with a mesh wide enough to hold only the biggest of catfish. It was an article of clothing that left everything to chance and nothing to the imagination. That was the moment the school bus happened by, the driver naturally slowing down for what looked like an emergency ahead. Every kid in the bus rushed to the windows to see what was going on. Sadly for Lance, it was a class from his high school returning home after a field trip to the Tyrell Museum in Drumheller. There wasn't a single kid on board who failed to recognize their very own high school hero, the quarterback from the Rams football team. A great cheer erupted, or was it a giant guffaw, as the bus crawled on by at forty clicks an hour. Lance could have, should have, would have jumped right back into his car, but the officer's words took him too much by surprise, stunned him almost.

"You can go now," she said, the smirk now unmistakable. "And in future, be a little more careful about who you hang out with." The slight emphasis on the words "hang out" forced her to turn away and regain her composure. Boy, she would have the mother of all traffic stories to tell the guys over coffee at Tim Horton's in an hour or so, that was for sure!

"I, I can go?" Lance was so disbelieving he had to ask the question to be sure he had heard right.

"That's what I said. Go, get out of here!"

Another vehicle slowed up as she said it, another gaggle of occupants staring in wonder at this almost nude hunk maybe modeling some new line of undergarment from "Victor's Secret", though there did not seem to be too much secrecy about it. The oversized, staring eyes galvanized Lance into action. Within seconds he was heading home, well within the speed limit, questions churning wildly in his mind. Why hadn't the cop charged him? Why hadn't she thrown the book at him? Why had she not even asked for his driver's license and insurance? Worse yet, how was he ever going to live this one down when so many had seen him standing there in all his glory? The answer, he was soon to find out, was that he would never live it down, not when some bright spark coined the nickname Knickers for him. In fact, the whole incident made him a much better person. It gave the kid humility where there had never been a trace of it before.

As for Katie, the spell had been broken and she knew it, accepted it with no small measure of relief. When she heard Lance storm out of the yard, she went over to the granary for some chop and called us. We were in the brush at the side of the driveway when we heard her, and we knew there was a treat at hand. We came back down the driveway and in through the barn door back to our pen. Kate gave us both a big hug and left with a telling few words. "Thank you, thank you both for giving me a lesson in life."

Maybe it was all the excitement. Maybe it was the disruption, but that night Pucky gave birth to a beautiful big bull calf, and she did it without help from anyone. The next morning Kate looked in before heading off to school. She was thrilled. "We'll call him Lance," she said. "No, PL, Poopy Lance." And so life moved on.

Chapter Ten

I Learn To Count

Pucky and PL were moved to make room for others, and I still waited—a day, three days, a week. I resembled a beached whale, even began to walk as a whale might walk if it sprouted legs. It was just as well that I hung on until a long weekend when the kids were home; otherwise, things could have turned out very differently. Saturday afternoon, and, oh, oh, here they come, those contractions that squeeze the bloody life out of you, literally and metaphorically. I lay down and got to work. Twenty minutes and ten mighty pushes later, and PLOP; the calf was out and I was on my feet. The little fellow was tiny, minute, half the size of PL, but I didn't care about size. He was mine and he was alive, quite weak it seemed, but alive. I got to work to give him a vigorous cleaning to get him going. He responded by desperately trying to get to his feet, but he just could not make it. I kept at him. Then Katie happened to pop in. As usual, she was hyper-thrilled. "Oh, Lucky," she cooed, "he's so tiny, but he's so beautiful." That was the trouble with Katie. If I had given birth to a toad, it would still have been "so beautiful". She had seen he was a he as soon as she came in. But he was still having a hard time getting up.

"I'll give you a bit more time," she said. "And I'll talk to Dad." That last phrase was decidedly ominous. The only human I would let fiddle around with my baby was Katie; as for Dad Carberry, why, I would have him up in the rafters as quick as look at him. After all, was he not the one who made Yucky disappear?

The conversation between Dad Carberry and his daughter was short and sweet. "Really tiny, you say? Then maybe we'd better check her out for twins," he said.

"Oh God, you know how spooked up she'll get," Katie responded. "You know how much she doesn't like you."

"Well now, that's too darn bad," he said. "You could very easily lose the twin if there is one, especially if it is backwards," he added, with that cold dash of icy logic that human dads always seem to exhibit. "It's your call. We can check her out or we can leave her alone. Your call, she's your cow. You have nothing to lose by checking her out though."

Which is why, when the barn door opened again, I knew I might be in some trouble because Katie was followed very purposefully by her dad. I gave him the evil eye as he made his way to the head-gate with a bucket of chop. Now I was schizoid, baby or chop, chop or baby, stomach or heart, empty stomach or bursting heart? With Katie urging me forward, chop won out. The second my head went through that head-gate to grab a bite of feed from the bucket, bingo, the closer snapped shut and I was trapped. I was trapped and very irate, wildly irate and pulling backwards with all my strength. No give, no choice, I wasn't going anywhere. Okay then, I might as well gorge myself on as much chop as I could. The moveable side gate now closed in, trapping me securely enough for human inspection.

"You do it. She's your cow." Dad Carberry was a hard taskmaster. "I'll hold on to her tail so she doesn't kick you." As if I would ever kick Katie!

Katie was one strong gal. She did not want to do it but she steeled herself. She inserted her arm into an elbow-length polythene glove, sweet-talking me all the time as she proceeded. I was oblivious. I knew it was Katie and besides, I had my head in the chop bucket, only pausing momentarily when I felt her hand touch my vulva. I shuddered but kept right on eating. Then I felt her hand slide in and I shuddered some more, but food was still my focus. The whoop of joy made me pause a good few seconds.

"Dad, dad, I feel a leg. Oh there's a leg Dad, and it moved. There's another baby in there, another baby, and it's still alive."

"Which way is it facing?" asked Mr. Stone Cold Logic.

"I don't know. I can't tell." The edge in her voice suggested she was close to panic.

"Sure you can tell. Think it through. Think of the shape. Think how a back leg bends and how a front leg bends."

Katie went back in. "Oh, oh, I feel its head, and an ear. I feel an ear."

"Good. Then it has to be facing the right way."

I had given up listening to their chatter, my mind being much too focused on chop, a treat I had not had since the day Lance spooked us.

"Now get a hold of both legs and line them up together." It was just as well Katie was now as tall as her father otherwise she would never have had the reach.

"Okay," she said, "but I don't think it's very big."

"It won't be, it's a twin, remember?" Mr. Cold Logic spoke again. "Now take this chain and loop it over the end of a foot like so."

Even though she was repulsed by all the blood and goop, Katie was a natural. Well, what would you expect? She was family. Although I have to admit, maybe it was empathy for the tiny being stuck inside my womb that forced her to stay the course.

"Got it," she gasped triumphantly.

"Now pull," said Macho Man Carberry not lifting a finger to help.

She pulled. A small hoof popped out, and then another, then two skinny little legs emerged.

"Put this second chain over the other leg and pull them both together." What was this? Did the Man Carberry see himself as some kind of indentured consultant?

Katie did as she was told. I stopped eating then, right at the point that the pressure built up, right at the moment when a pink nose appeared followed by a head with two great big unblinking eyes and the front shoulders. Katie gave an extra big pull and calf and all flopped out onto her as she lost her balance and keeled over backwards. There she lay, momentarily stunned, a tiny calf lying on top of her. Surprisingly now, she was not in the least fazed by the mess nor by the amateurish way her pull had concluded; she was Katie, my Katie, crying joyfully, joyfully crying. Who knew what she was doing, anyway, when she didn't know herself?

Dad Carberry gently lifted the tiny calf off his daughter and carried it over to her brother, having first noted that this one was a she. Then he threw some of the remnants of the amniotic fluid over him so that they both smelled the same and so hopefully both would be cleaned off by me. To further assure an equal interest, he took the remainder of my chop and scattered it over the babies. He knew me for sure. I would lick the chop off both; I'd do anything for chop.

"I'm outa here," he announced grandly. "You go ahead and let her out, but for heaven's sake be careful. I'll be waiting for you outside." Now was this a tacit recognition of his daughter's competence from a loving father, or what?

Katie came over to me. Instinctively, I sniffed at the goop on her clothes and knew instantly that she was on my side, she was working for me. She released the catch on the head-gate and I backed out to go looking for my baby. WHOA! Now there were two babies where before there had only been one: two brown "tinies" with great big eyes and floppy ears. I began my business once more, licking the chop off one and then the other, barely looking up when Kate stepped out through the door.

As I keep telling you, humans have this thing about numbers. We don't. We cows have no need to count everything, all our money, all our possessions; we have no need to figure out our net worth and balance our budgets. If we had ever needed to do that, our brains would have been wired appropriately or the farmers would have given us each a calculator when we reached puberty. For me "One is one, and all and all, and ever more shall be so," as the old song goes. So counting all the way up to two was not something I was born to do. You need to understand this as psychological background for my behaviour, and so that you forgive me. You see, both of my babies were weak, as twins often are. But the one was a good deal weaker and less pushy than the other. No guessing which of the two was the weaker one! Males of any and all species are generally "the slow boats to China", the late developers and the sluggish bloomers. Why, I would even venture to suggest that some of them don't ever bloom. It was the male who was the first born, and yet it was the male who had the most difficulty getting going. Perhaps he had been too cramped in the womb. Perhaps he was lacking something, vitamins or minerals, selenium perhaps. But when Katie popped in an hour later, it was the female that was up suckling. The same female she had pulled into this world on the end of a chain, the same again that Katie was convinced would be handicapped because of all the added trauma. I admit it now; if Katie had not intervened when she did, I would have left the male to fend for himself. After all, I had a calf, a live and suckling calf, so what more did I need? Remember now, cows can only count to one.

I watched Katie gently lift the male onto his feet. She hobbled him over to where I was standing and put a tit into his mouth. I was not particularly happy about this, but I let it pass since it was dear Katie who was directing operations. The little beast was hungry, voracious even. With Katie holding him up on his feet, he sucked at that tit as if there might be no tomorrow. She tried letting him go to see if the blood was circulating enough to let him stand on his own. He crashed unceremoniously to the ground, and try as he might, he could not get back up. Again, Katie picked him up; again Katie brought him in to nurse, and nurse he sure did, cleaning one quarter out almost entirely. There was no way he could manage another for I carried far too much milk. Still, both babies had now got a belly full of life-giving colostrum. You could quite easily hear their bellies gurgling in fullness. Katie carried the male over to a clean patch of bedding and then shepherded the female over to join him. Completely satiated, they settled into deep sleep, cuddled up together.

Now Katie turned on me. "Now you listen up, Luck. You look after both of those babies, you hear me?" She would have made a great grandmother, my Kate, or even a Mother Superior at a convent. "Especially the little guy cuz he doesn't have much oomph. He needs time, and you, you need patience." I fidgeted uncomfortably. She came over and patted me reassuringly before throwing me a thick wad of alfalfa hay that she took out of the bale store. Okay, okay, no need to get on my case, I would do what she wanted, I was thinking.

"Oh, and I've got the names for your babies. The girl is Teeter and the boy is Totter, okay? So you'd better darn well look after them."

Four hours later one calf stirred and woke the other. Teeter the female was up on her feet right away and ready to go exploring for a tit. "Totter" did what his name suggested; he tottered to his feet and then willed himself to take a step, barely a success. He wobbled there for a good twenty seconds before managing another step, then another and another. The moment he presumed to touch my tit with his cold nose, I floored him with a head butt. I could only count to one, and that "one" was on my other side, guzzling furiously. "Totter" lay there confused before once again regaining his feet. The door happened to open just as he tried for a tit, and a horrified Katie saw me floor him once more. I had never seen Katie mad, but now she was mad. Oh, she was hopping mad. Never before had she ever whacked me, but this was one time when she did, a real whack from the pink cane that she had taken from its nail on the wall. I bolted to the corner leaving "Totter" to suddenly wonder where on earth his tit had gone. Now, when I get mad, humans get scared. When Katie got mad, I was the one who got scared. There I was, a fourteen hundred pound cow intimidated by a one hundred and ten pound girl. Gently she picked up poor old "Totter" and rubbed his legs vigorously. Then she gave him a slew of shots—vitamin and selenium and scour preventative and who knows what all else—all designed to get his system in gear. Then she ordered me into the head-gate, and I went as meek as could be. I was not about to defy my Katie when she was on the warpath, no way! She came over and snapped the mechanism shut, talking to me softly and rubbing me behind the ear.

"Now you listen up, Lucky dear, and you listen good. Right this minute, and right from this minute on, you're gonna damn well learn how to count to two." This was Katie talking, my Katie. Not Katie pretending to be a grandma, but Katie talking with Gronk-style lingo. Yet she wasn't threatening so much as soothing. That's how I knew I was in tough. "See, you've gotta understand; you gave birth to two, you raise two. That's all there is to it." People who say animals don't understand what people are saying to them had better think again. Maybe we don't always understand the actual words, but we are quick to get the message

I heard, and then saw out of the corner of my eye, Katie bring "Totter" over to me. I felt that tiny mouth latch onto my tit, and instinctively I let loose the mother of all kicks, just grazing Katie's knee. I had never done anything like that before to her, never, but she and the Thing were invading my space, and darn it, was I not entitled to let her know that? Like really!

That was the only other time she ever whacked me in anger. Something in my brain told me I should be ashamed, but I wasn't quite sure what I was supposed to be ashamed about. Katie wasted no time. Gently she took "Totter" back to his spot and stormed out of the barn. I should have known what she was up to. She came back with *El Toro*, and *El Toro* Carberry knew exactly how to handle a hostile cow, especially one with which he had had issues before. He tied my one back leg to a post with a stout rope. Katie came up to my head to talk to me, but I was in the foulest of moods. I shook my head and blew snot at her and she walked away. Then together, father and daughter walked "Totter" over to me, gave him a tit and again he sucked ravenously, his tail wagging like a pendulum in a hurry. I tried one more kick, a real doozie, and I near broke my back because I had forgotten my leg was still tied to the post. So I gathered myself together and suffered in silence, my own tail flicking madly from one side to the other to express my anger.

Okay, so both calves were now full. They would let me out and I could get on with my life, and if the Thing came near me again, I would flatten him again, or so I thought.

"Leave her in there. If she wants to learn to count to two the hard way, then I guess that's what she wants to do." *El Toro* didn't have a single empathetic vein in his body.

"Really? Do you think that's a good idea?" Katie almost rallied to my defense.

"It's a really good idea," replied Hitler's brother. "She'll soon figure out that either she does her job untied or she does it tied up. Come on, let's you and I go have a game of Scrabble. We'll come back up after I've beaten you."

"As if!" Katie retorted, moving both calves back to their sleeping spot. Amazingly, "Totter" walked there, if a mite unsteadily.

They released me an hour and a half later and fed me more hay and a handful of chop. But I was in no mood to be grateful; I was too busy indulging in an Olympic size sulk. The calves showed no interest, so they were left alone to sleep. "We'll check in on you again at ten o'clock," Dad Carberry confided to me before they left.

Kate looked in on me at nine. She saw both calves up, so she closed the door quietly and stood outside watching me through a crack in the wall. She saw Teeter latch onto a tit, saw "Totter" endeavor to do the same, and saw me push him away. She burst into that barn like a runaway circus elephant. With no backup, no support troops, no WBD, Weapons of Bovine

Destruction, she marched me back into the head-gate and secured it. She herself tied my kicking foot to the post with the sort of knot a beginning Girl Guide might not be too proud of, and then she ushered the two babies up to the buffet. Both pigged out, both ended up with bellies so bulging, they looked as if they might suddenly float up into the air like a pair of hot air balloons. Not a word crossed her lips, not a friendly gesture broke the tension; it was hard-core silent treatment all the way. Once the two young'uns had lost interest, she took them back to their neutral corner. That was when she astounded me, and cut me to the quick all at the same time.

"So long, you bitch!" she said using one of those hated five-letter Gronkspeak words that I never thought I would hear her use, and it was directed at me. "You can stay there all night, bitch!" Well, there was no mistaking who had run out of her high cards!

By two in the morning, I was feeling sort of contrite. By three in the morning, I was considering surrender. By four, I might even have let "Totter" suckle unmolested. By five, when Kate showed up, I was beaten. I was aching all over, my kicking leg had gone numb, and my anger had long since drained away into the ethers of history. Without a word, without a pat on the rump, Kate let me out. I could barely stand, I was so sore. Kate got the calves up. "Totter" was nearly as quick on his feet as his sister. And I let them both go at it; it had been a long, hard lesson but I had finally learned to count to two.

At that moment, Dad Carberry, *El Toro* himself, stumbled through the door to find his precious little daughter in control of all she surveyed. "You're just like your mother," he said. "Why didn't you call me?" he asked, rubbing sleep from his eyes.

"Call you? What for? What were you gonna do?"

"You could have been killed. That's one big cow, you know, and she can be ornery. She's had more than one go at me, remember?"

"I didn't need you, Dad," Katie said sweetly. "She's my cow and I trust her. Besides, I can run way faster than you, Dad, so don't sweat it."

For most animals, but I suspect for humans especially, there comes a day when their offspring demonstrate a superior competency at business than those who sired and raised them. Such a day was fast approaching for Dad Carberry, *El Toro*.

Shirley Jackson

Chapter Eleven

Of Whippet & Toy Boys

Let me tell you something for nothing, for free, gratis! If humans believe the cost of raising twins is horrendous, they need to try suckling them for as long as we have to. As with humans, I'm sure, it's so often the smaller specimens who eat more, and in my own case, more often. Once Teeter and Totter had figured out that the meaning of life lay in what they ate, and how often, their appetites seemed to know no bounds, and as their appetites bloomed, so did their vigor. They couldn't just look for a tit. No, they had to come barreling in and then fight over it. Oh sure, I had four functional tits and a near perfect udder, so the milk was equally distributed. But these twins behaved like humans for whom possession is nine-tenths of the law. If one of them had claimed a particular tit, let's say the left front, the other had to have it at all cost. So it became a routine, the shoving and the bunting, the civil war that went on between them, which in a way was why their names were somehow appropriate, Teeter-Totter. When one was up, the other was down. Yet, they were also inseparable; for as much as they fought each other for food, outside of meal times they were buddies. Even I came to see them as one, so in a sense, my lessons in counting were unlearned. Probably because they had started out life so tiny, I was more protective of them than I had been of any of my offspring. It was uncanny, too, that when Katie was around, they acted like her pet poodles, trotting along at her heels whenever she appeared. She always had a sugar lump for them; probably not good for their teeth, but what did I know, I was only their mother. Come to think of it, maybe that was why they were so hyper. Too much sugar!

This particular year, winter could not make up its mind whether to stay or go. Just when things looked like they were warming up, another bout of igloo weather would blow in. It was downright depressing. If it hadn't been for their newly constructed calf houses, the Carberry Spread would have buried more than a few calves. The twins had it all figured out though; they had their own special place in the back of one of the calf sheds and they defended it robustly against all comers. More than once I saw them bully a calf twice their size from their favourite spot. Actually, it was just after one of these bitter blow-ins that Whippet went and cast herself. I had never ever seen this phenomenon. It was one of those rare occurrences when a cow tips over the wrong way perhaps trying to lick at an itch on her back, and then she finds she cannot right herself. This time it was Mike, not Katie, who made the call, and he came up big.

Mike always did the night check on Fridays and Saturdays in calving season, giving his frazzled parents the chance to rest up. On this particular night, he had returned late from a get-together with his friends so he went straight up to the corrals when he got home. Techno Man Dad had rigged up enough in the way of lighting to make the place look like New York's Times Square at New Year's when you switched the lights on. In addition, Mike also carried a powerful spotlight that he shone into the corners and any areas of shadow. There, in one of the corrals in a slight dip in the ground lay Whippet, a very distressed Whippet, a Whippet who was clearly dying. To begin with, Mike did not know what to make of it, he had never experienced such a thing before, but he knew right away that something was radically wrong. What he did not know was that without intervention, Whippet would be dead in twenty minutes. The sheer weight of her body was crushing the life out of her lungs, her body shape preventing her from rolling back up to save herself. Part of the shape issue was due to the fact she had not yet calved. Okay, so what should he do? Wake up the old man of course!

As soon as Dad Carberry's mind tore itself from a golf game in the company of Playboy's Miss November, 1989, he knew he had to get up, even if his brain was so reluctant to let go the image of an over-endowed playmate wearing not much more than a stylized bunny tail and a Santa Claus hat, both clearly intended to keep sensitive regions warm while golfing in the snow.

"Sounds like she has cast herself," said Tiger Carberry. "We've got to get her up or she will die. C'mon, let's see if you and I and Mom can push her up."

"Wha', what's going on?" echoed Mama Carberry's sleepy voice, as she was woken by all of the commotion. Her mind was reluctant to let go of the image of playing golf with George Clooney, or was it Robert Redford, or maybe it was the local MLA. Whoever it was—and that in itself was hard to read because the face kept switching—was dressed in the robes of Simba the Lion King. Was there some sort of subliminal message here, or what? No time to find out. She was press-ganged out of bed, but at least they spared Katie.

When they got back to poor old Whippet, they saw clearly they did not have much time. So desperate were they, they did not stop to think.

It was just as well Mike had taken up the sport of judo, and just as well he had made a point of perfecting the landing technique once he had been thrown. He rushed in to help his Whippet, grabbing her back leg with the intention of pulling her backwards. Instantly she pulled her leg forwards, dragging Mike with it, and then let go with a mighty kick surely destined to send Mike after the cow that jumped over the moon. His trajectory alone was impressive enough, the distance he traveled doubly so, while the technique he used to land on frozen ground was, well, bone-saving if not life-saving. Somehow, he had been able to curl up like a ball and land like a cat; nobody knew quite how he managed it. For his mother who was watching, he was undoubtedly a goner. To his father, he couldn't possibly walk away from this one. But he did, even if he used a cuss word that his mother could not bring herself to critique in the circumstances. And Whippet continued to lie there in deep distress. What were these humans thinking? How could two of them, ten percent below prime, and one of them, Mike, ten percent above prime even think they could roll over a fourteen hundred pound cow?

"I'll go get the tractor," said Dad Carberry with his usual stone cold logic.

"It has a flat front tire, remember?" said Mama Carberry, most unhelpfully.

"Well, the other tractor won't start," said Dad. "We have no choice. Murphy's Law."

The Murphy's Law that Jim Carberry was referring to was always applicable to farming. It went something like this: "That which you do not want to happen *will happen for sure, and with compound interest.*" The fact that the front tire was worn out years ago represented the compound interest in this instance.

Now getting a tractor with a flat front tire from Point A to Point B via three sharp left turns, two sharp rights, and two gates in between represents a challenge. Add the darkness of a moonless night and the speed required in a life-and-death emergency coupled with the resolve of a farmer to rescue his cow, and you get the picture; a lopsided tractor with only one working light driven by a representative of *Humanitas Insanitas* thumping his foot first on the right brake and then on the left to make the monster turn.

Faith Carberry knew her husband. She turned to Mike. "Son, would you go down to the shop and grab the tow sling hanging on the south wall. I hung it there yesterday, so I know your father has not yet had the time to lose it. I can tell you now, and I'll give you a hundred dollars if I'm wrong, he won't have remembered to bring it with him. Hurry."

Mike left in the hurry he needed to execute. He could care less about the hundred dollars. He had to save Whippet—his cow, his very first cow—and he was certain that they had only minutes to save her, if her laboured breathing was anything to go by. Faith opened the corral gate and her husband lurched in, the flip-flop of the front tire peeling off the rim spooking the remaining cows into a far corner. Oh, but Dad Carberry was good, very good, a real tractor boy. In one wild move, he spun that iron monster around so that he ended up facing away from Whippet's rump, just the way he needed to be. He didn't feel it yet because there was too much adrenalin pumping, but his shoulders ached, his feet ached; his whole body was one big ache. He got out of the cab, although fell out would have been closer to the mark.

"Shit, I forgot the sling! Shit! Faith, do you happen to know where...?" "Hush little baby, don't say a word, if you happen to fall down, you'll fall in a turd." God she could be so...condescending. No, that was worse than condescending! "It's on its way, courtesy of Mikey Express."

Mike appeared seconds later with the sling. Gingerly avoiding the repeat possibility of a kick, he slipped the loop of the sling over a back leg. He need not have worried. Whippet couldn't have managed a kick even if she had wanted. Dad Carberry hitched the other end to the drawbar before climbing back into the tractor and slipping it into gear. The sling tightened, the cow let loose a deep bellow and then she began to move, sliding along the frozen ground on her side. The depression in which she had cast herself was shaped like a very shallow saucer, but it had been enough. Dad Carberry came to a stop then backed up to loosen the tension on the sling. Before Mike could make a move to get the sling off her foot, Whippet had struggled unsteadily to her feet. She stood there shaking and gulping in huge lungfuls of air, and regarding the whole world about her with hostile eyes, as if the humans had all been somehow responsible for her predicament. Even Mike realized how foolhardy it would have been to go in and try to remove the sling from her foot. He didn't have the same kind of relationship with Whippet as Katie had with me. To him, Whippet was more of a commercial holding. As they held their breath and watched, Whippet turned round and the sling loosened. With her first two steps forward, it dropped away and she headed for the bale feeder, with not a single thank-you nod, not a shred of gratitude, not even a forced smile at her rescuers.

"Thanks Mom, thanks Dad," said Mike quietly. "You guys just saved my cow."

"You had a lot to do with it, son," replied Mama. "C'mon, let's all go back to bed. We've still got half the night to dream through."

Of course, she could never have known why her last comment put an extra spring in her husband's step, just as much as he should have known the image of his pet bunny had long ago skipped away to greener pastures, likely George Clooney or Robert Redford.

Before I forget, I have to tell you that three days later Whippet gave birth to another monster bull calf that Katie, with her ineffable logic, named Flippit. To Katie, every living thing deserved a name just so that it had an identity.

Finally the winter became a memory. The schizophrenic spring morphed into summer, and once again we were back on pasture. Except that this year, Whippet and I, and ten or so others, were kept at home. For the first year ever, I didn't get shipped out to rented land. I didn't care that much really, but I was a little apprehensive at the beginning, a little suspicious of why our group was being held back. Had we done something wrong? Call it paranoia if you want, but I had to be convinced we were not being saved for somebody's meat-grinder or the auction mart. It all became horribly clear when we saw the new bull. Bathtub, the Black Angus bull, had gone out to the rented pasture with the main herd. We were the ones designated to get "new blood".

We saw and heard the stock trailer rattle up to the pasture gate, saw Mama Carberry open it and drive through. (By way of explanation, as a rule macho dads don't open gates because they're too busy displaying their virility driving truck and trailer with one hand, the other hanging out of the window.) We watched with extreme suspicion. Were we about to be rounded up and shipped off to dog-food heaven? We saw Dad Carberry open the trailer door, and out HE walked; not "he" as in "him" but H.E. as in His Excellency. And no, it was not so much that he walked as strutted with all of the arrogance of an heir to the throne; his muscles rippling, and coat shining. Heavens above, it was like us girls watching "The Bachelor" on T.V!

I have to say, up until now I had always kept my distance from bulls, most bulls that is, but this one…well! He was a Shorthorn, a purebred Shorthorn. "So what?" you might say. Remember my daddy was the neighbor's Shorthorn that jumped the fence and gave my mother something to think about: me. Don't get me wrong now. I am not a racist, and I'm not xenophobic, but this was my own kind, and at this moment in time, I preferred my own kind, especially when my own kind was this… stunning, this…spectacular. I couldn't help myself; I was the one to lead the charge to check him out. He came to a stop and just stood there, secure in his majesty. He was the pop star to whom all the groupies were gravitating, tossing their personals at him as they drew nigh. He was the most regal of kings, and we were the lowly courtiers dazzled by his sheer nobility. He was the supreme champion of "So You Think You Can Dance, Canada," and we were auditioning to be his partner. He was much younger than most of us, but he had presence beyond his years. He sported the roan colouring unique to the Shorthorn breed—mottled browns and reds dappled with white—and he had a head and a neck that brashly proclaimed all he stood for, from tip of nose to end of tail. Our excitement was palpable, our flattery of him downright shameful, but he was ours, all ours. He was our very own toy boy whom we all loved instantly and often. His name could have been Flatfoot Invader XXVI for all we cared, but it wasn't; it was Greenacres WhizKid, WhizKid in name, and all WhizKid in fame!

It was not surprising that the first three weeks of his presence were so frenetic. It was not surprising that every cow in the group had been bred, some of us several times just for the fun of it. He was like a movie mogul working his way through a bevy of starlets. And reminiscent of my father, when he was done with us, he jumped the fence and happily bred ten or so of the neighbor's purebred Charolais cows; cows from one of the premier Charolais breeders in the province. Oh those neighbor folks were not happy when they found him, not happy one little tiny bit. Worse still, WhizKid had run off a much bigger Charolais bull named Taliban and had taken over his girls while Taliban sulked under a willow bush. They got WhizKid out for sure, but they were aghast at the results the following year when a string of what should have been fullblood Charolais prospects appeared wearing the roan colours of their daddy's favourite team. (Their anger dissipated in the fall when the calves were weaned. Hybrid vigor generated top prices and heavy weights, so their human obsession with numbers was amply rewarded.) But Techno Dad Carberry was compelled to install a double wire electric fence to keep young Whiz at home. Just as well, for now he had time to recoup all of the weight he had lost from his gallivanting about the country. By fall, he was once again awesome to behold.

Ah, but I have to tell you, there was divine retribution for the Carberry installation of that electric fence, even if the retribution was visited upon one of the more innocent of the family; Mama Carberry, the one Carberry with whom I had never had a rumble. The module that powered the fence was solar-operated. It was affixed to a corner brace, with the panel facing the sun. The on-off switch was located beneath the module; you had to crawl underneath to press it in for "on" and pull it out for "off". You have to know these technical details in order to fully understand what happened next.

Mom and Dad Carberry had driven up to check the line; for the sake of good neighborly relations, they could not risk the bull getting out again. Jim's cell phone sounded just as he was about to get out of the truck, so he stayed put to take the call while Faith went on alone. Along the way, she came upon a shrub touching the wire, could hear it clicking and knew that the sound represented a serious draw down, on power and zap. It being summer and hot, she was dressed for the summer heat: short skirt, summer blouse, light and breezy all the way. She went over to the module and switched the machine off. Then she walked back along the fence line and stomped the offending bush into the ground before returning to the module to switch on. She had to bend down to remind herself where the switch was, and she switched it on. It was in straightening up that her forehead touched the live wire. There was a shriek that no human being should ever make: a shriek that caused every bird, beast, and insect within half a mile to stop whatever it was doing and assume a defensive posture. And there was Mama Carberry, flat out on the ground, knickers to the sun, wondering if she had been suddenly struck by divine retribution for all her mortal sins. The answer could probably be summed up by a line from the great book, "Bovinius Classicus Vivendi": "…for the sins of the farmer are never visited upon himself but upon his spouse and his progeny. For what shall it profit such a man if in all his deviousness, he should be the direct recipient of such striking consequences as to lay him low…" Mama Carberry was too stunned to decide yet just how unhappy she was, but Dad Carberry was now out of the truck and found himself close enough to revel in the view. Then he started to laugh, and laughed so hard he had to sit down on the ground. Now, Faith was a bit like me; she was not one to be laughed at. She came to at that laughter, looked around, and spotted a half-dry cow-pie. Big Dada was still blind with laughter when that soggy projectile caught him about the ear. What then ensued was a demonstration of how low humanity can go as a genuine full-blown shit fight erupted between two soon to be revolting protagonists. There was cow poop in hair, on clothes, everywhere. They couldn't even drive home; they had to walk, they were so disgusting!

Chapter Twelve   Big Whiz

Beware the quad, that's what we all said. The sound of the quad too often signified something ominous, like a roundup or incarceration or vaccination. Whenever we saw it approaching, we would do a heads-up to contemplate whether we needed to run to the far reaches of wherever we were. However, we also discovered that we could never outrun it; and worse yet, if the driver was a male specimen of *Genius Humanitas*, then you could easily end up with the quad's steel rack ramming you hard up the ass. I tried taking it on a couple of times, but take it from me, it is nigh impossible to kick and run at the same time, even for a nimble-footed cow. And you know me; I always had to try at least one kick. So we always made a point of seeing who was driving. If it was either one of the H-O-W Carberrys, "Hell-On-Wheels Carberrys", we automatically switched into retreat mode. If it were Mama Carberry or Katie, they would likely be bumbling along at granny speed, delivering mineral to a feeder or checking a gate, or just coming to see how we were doing. For this, we remained only on amber alert.

The day came that fall when the Carberry herd out on rental pasture was trucked home. Now, whenever components of the same overall herd are separated and then brought back together after a substantial time apart, the whole blessed game of reestablishing the hierarchy comes into play. So the fifty cows that arrived back that afternoon had to be "officially welcomed" by us stay-at-home moms, while our offspring took off on their own catch-me-if-you-can game around the pasture. With that came my first big surprise; the twins were as big and hunky as any of the other calves. Broad in the beam and heavy in the muscle, they could hold their own with any of the newcomers. The second surprise was that they off-loaded Bathtub the Black Angus bull with the cows, along with a young sidekick by the name of Ulysses. If cows are compelled to fight to show their ascendancy, bulls are far worse, and Black Angus was reputedly worse than any. Bathtub took one malevolent look at WhizKid and the fight was on. This, in turn, muted our own jockeying for power, for a good bullfight is not a spectacle you want to miss. I have to say, I had forgotten how ugly Bathtub was. He was fearsome and big, yes, but big on the side of sluggish, which meant that like an over-handicapped racehorse, he was carrying too much ballast.

WhizKid knew no fear. He simply stood stock still on a slight rise in the ground and dared the other two to come and take him. U-U as we later called him, Useless Ulysses, too aggressively obliged and faked a charge. But, however much Ulysses was useless in our eyes, he was smart. As he closed in on WhizKid, it dawned on him that, gosh darn it, he had maybe bitten off a bit more than he could chew. His charge tapered off into one of those "hello-and-how-the-hell-are-you" encounters of the neo-polite kind. Indeed, you could almost see it crossing his mind as he checked out this formidable Shorthorn fighting machine that he would do better to rethink his allegiance to Bathtub.

Clearly, the subservient behaviour of his junior pushed Bathtub over the top. Snorting loudly and stopping to paw out another chunk of ground, he bellowed his best defiance. WhizKid never moved. Okay, enough was enough; he would show this young stud who was going to be undisputed boss. He approached warily. WhizKid stayed put. Like a general who knew that in battle timing is everything, he waited, biding his time. This strategy had a marked psychological effect on Bathtub. He could see that he, Bathtub, had the advantage of size and weight, yet this young whippersnapper remained strangely unimpressed. This, in front of all the cows watching, his cows dammit! He put his massive head down in a mock charge, his enormous hooves digging up great clods of dirt as he completed his show of intimidation. Adult humans generally know this. Poopy Lance discovered it at great cost: if you are working too hard at projecting a particular image, you can miss critical signals being generated around you. WhizKid saw his moment had arrived. He launched himself like a heat-seeking missile locked on target.

Bathtub's head was not quite where he would have wanted it in an all-out fight. Committed to his bluff, he had not expected close quarters combat to happen quite so quickly, and he was almost knocked off his feet. *War of the Worlds, Clash of the Titans*, "The Battle of Carberry Plain", any one of those descriptors would have suited just fine. Very quickly, though, Bathtub got the message that he was seriously outclassed by a much younger bull: a bull fully in his prime. He had never read any work entitled "The Inescapable Laws of Nature", or another entitled "Reality Really Sucks". He had never learned that there comes a day in the life of any bull when he shall be unseated from his throne by a young upstart, a virile usurper in a game of "winner takes all the ladies". WhizKid was incredibly fast and nimble on his feet, exceptionally good at feinting and then withdrawing unscathed, very adept at building up his opponent's frustrations and wearing him down.

Bathtub weighed about twenty-three hundred pounds; WhizKid came in somewhere around nineteen hundred pounds. Carrying those extra four hundred pounds would ordinarily have assured the heavier bull certain victory, but only if he asserted his superiority at the outset. Bathtub didn't and then Bathtub couldn't. After ten minutes, it was all over. Bathtub breaking off in surrender and desperate at least to regain at least some of his breath, forgot about his dignity. All the new girls crowded around WhizKid who clearly reveled in their attention. Even U-U came to pay his respects, only for WhizKid to make it very apparent that he wasn't into male hangers-on.

As for poor old Bathtub, he put on one more show for us a day later, but WhizKid ran rings around him. Actually not that old for a breeding bull coming up to five years old, from then on, Bathtub acted like a "has-been", a retired blue-collar worker without a hobby. We couldn't miss it, nor did the Carberrys. Whatever interest he had once shown in his job evaporated. There were one or two cows still cycling, but Bathtub wasn't the slightest bit interested. He was like an over-the-hill sex bomb whose fuse had fizzled. The only thing he could raise was a scowl. It was WhizKid who stepped up to the plate and took care of necessities; a bit of a waste, really, because any cows still cycling at that time of the year were obviously not very fertile and would be culled. And for Bathtub, his retirement routine became his swan song. Jim Carberry knew that as a breeding bull, Beelzebub or Bathtub was all washed up. Attitude is always the Great Betrayer, and Bathtub's attitude was now all about laid-back leisure before carnal pleasure. He, too, was shipped with the culled cows. Okay, so the Carberrys would be in the market for a bull the following spring.

Not again! Surely not again! My heart stopped when I looked up from the grain feeder. Yep, there they were, and *two* of them were on quads. Every gate was manned. And like riot police when they get the signal, they began to advance, *Genius Humanitas* with an agenda. The docile old bags among us headed up towards the corral as planned. Not me, no sir. Not me, not Teeter, and not Totter. We made a break for it. I knew where there was a weak spot in the fence, a spot where the wire hung low because a couple of staples were missing. Even though I was fast, I should have known that it wasn't going to be Mama Carberry on the quad but her teenaged son. The combination of male teenager invincibility and high speed could only have meant one thing; Mr. Invincible would get to wherever I was going before me. Young Mike also possessed "cow sense";

he could read exactly what I was thinking and react accordingly. Hollering away in great excitement, he easily turned us back, and within minutes we were in the corral with the rest of those docile old wussies, waiting to have their babies taken away. Yes, it was weaning time again—weaning and sale time—and the tale of the twins, like the tale of Yucky before them, came to an abrupt end. There was no sparing either of them; both were consigned to a feedlot somewhere down near Medicine Hat.

Here is a mathematical principle I learned that day. If the weaning of twins stops double the drain, (on my body you understand), their absence from my life doubled the pain. Yes, I had learned to see them and treat them as one; weaning them re-divided that one into the memory of two. Oh how I missed them, pined for them, ached for them so hard that I believed no tomorrow would let me move on. But again, the sheer functionality of living finally dulled the senses and coaxed back the necessary reacceptance of my bovine reality. We were put on this earth to reproduce and provide a rich source of protein to a superior being. That was our lot, our fate, and our destiny. Yes, we could experience so many of the emotions experienced by humans—hate, love, greed and lust— but we were and are a commercial commodity, nonetheless. We are the numbers in somebody's bottom line, we are "the fats and the culls, the backgrounders and the grassers", we are steak on the hoof and roast in the pot.

On into fall and then into winter did we soldier; "soldier" being the operative word. The cold was bitter, the unrelenting wind was biting, and the endeavor to keep warm was constant. Thank heaven the Carberrys had kept their trees despite the persistent efforts from some hard-hats in the logging fraternity to add sweet-sounding numbers to their farm income with an offer to fell all their trees, the big spruce in particular, and buy all the lumber. Thank heaven trees were sacred to Faith and Jim Carberry; so sacred that no lumberman's silvery tongue could shake them. And so we cows had as good a place as any to shelter when so many bovines in the province had to survive an open landscape. Even then, when we were not eating, we were numb. But at least with the trees, we could always find a spot to stand or lie down in the lee of a poplar or a spruce. It was not that we actually knew we were better off. While this winter's cold was so uncompromising, the wind chill was far worse because it sought us out to taunt us. It percolated into the deepest marrow of our bones, and there we were, hallucinating about the green grass of summer pastures and believing that never again would we ever get warm. We endured a week, two weeks, a full month before the weather finally broke and the sun radiated its smile.

Humans so spoil themselves with their heating and their air conditioning, they truly do not resonate to the climate like we do. When it gets cold, they reach for their so-called long-johns or their woollen-annies. They insulate with thinsulate, they jump into a hot tub or curl up beside a warm fire, and there we are, out there in the elements, our tits even freezing to the ground on occasion. Anything that hangs down is susceptible to frostbite, which was why I was so glad I wasn't a bull in winter. I mean it's not as if they have any choice, they always have to leave their bag of groceries outside the door. I was one of those cows who preferred to stand because it was better for the circulation. Getting down to take the weight off the feet was one thing, getting back up was quite another, especially when your limbs are so numb they will not respond. But standing all the time took its toll, too. Hour after hour, you would stand there inducing yourself into a sort of trance, only breaking out of it when hunger sent a message down to your feet to come to life and head over to the feeders for a bite of hay. Pucky and I were both lucky. Why wouldn't I be lucky with the name I had been given? We developed our own version of grandma's winter coat because the hair on our hides grew thick and woolly. Not so poor old Whippet. Her hair was too fine, so she suffered far more from the cold than we ever did.

Humans and their accursed economics baffle me, always will. There never seems to be any sense of contentment or satisfaction with things as they are. If business is not in expansion mode, then it is in contraction mode: expansion good, contraction bad. As if that is not enough, humans then have to invent a plethora of regulations, and no matter what happens, they always complicate business further. Their taxation system is a case in point. They do certain things to get a "tax write-off," and then they do certain other things to reduce the tax bill at the end of the year. They don't want any of their tax money going to the common good, no way! So livestock farmers buy critters in December; a grain farmer will buy a new machine, a combine, or a tractor. And so it was with the Carberrys. After a pretty good year, more off the farm than on it, they did not want to pay more tax than they needed, and they were in expansion mode, which is why twenty more bred cows suddenly appeared on the farm just before Christmas. The Carberrys had gone to a dispersal sale at Olds Auction Mart, more out of curiosity than with any grand intention to buy. The market signals of man's economics can be read a multiple of ways. In this case, the seller had decided that he had had enough of what he considered mediocre prices for his product, so he was calling it a day and going fishing. What the hell, the market could decide what he was worth…and it did, oh it sure did! He got little better than fire sale prices for a beautiful set of cows. People are always on hand to snap up a bargain, and the Carberrys were no exception. They bought twenty, the quality of the cows being as good as any they had seen in a long time. The fact that they all came from the same herd meant that there was less chance of importing in some unpronounceable disease like Johne's onto the farm.

So twenty Gelbvieh-influenced, barrel-shaped cows arrived just before the Christmas lights were switched on, and the jockeying for position and influence had to begin all over again. Happily, there wasn't too much to it this time because these girls were still young and impressionable. They were also heavily in calf, scheduled to calve in early March. It was WhizKid who screwed it all up and got himself into the Carberry's bad books. He heard all of the commotion and broke out of his own designated bullpen to check things out. Two thousand-plus pounds of prime rib doth not an Olympic show-jumper make. He broke the top two boards of the plank fence and brought U-U out with him. It was not as if they could rampantly sow their seed or anything. Every cow in the herd was both bred and not in the least bit interested; not a happy scenario for a couple of young studs on the prowl, looking for a bit of action. But the affair did conspire to give the two Carberry macho men a lesson in life, young Macho Mike especially.

When a bull, particularly a young bull, is trolling for a spot of J-J, "Jumping Jemimah", he resents interference from any outside source. He is after all fulfilling his *raison d'être*, his reason for living, so he goes about his quest with purpose. Unfortunately, on this day, bovine purpose conflicted with human purpose; specifically, the intention of the Carberrys to get the bulls back into their pen just as quickly as they could. First they repaired the fence and then went to fetch the bulls. Now, WhizKid was always an obliging fellow. He was cooperative because he almost certainly knew that there was not a single female out there receptive to his advances. Truth be told, he might just as well have broken into a nunnery. Not so with Useless Ulysses: he was motivated, excited, so over-excited, in fact, that he tried to mount a bewildered Whippet from the wrong end. Young Mike approached him on the quad, trying to deflect his attention away from the unwilling object of his desire. Whether it was the threat of the cane Mike was carrying or the noise of the quad, nobody would ever know for sure. But U-U suddenly turned on Mike, stuck his head underneath the machine's frame and rolled it over like a dog playing with a new toy. Mike was now pinned beneath it and highly vulnerable to further attack when Dad Carberry came screaming to the rescue, waving a length of two by four. Never in his life had he moved so fast, never in his life would he move so fast again. He whacked that bull full across the muzzle, and that same bull was an instant convert to a new philosophy of peace and understanding. Dad Carberry moved quickly over to his son and lifted the quad off him while the bull retreated.

"Are you okay, son?" Dad panted.

"Yeah, I'm okay. Pissed off, but okay. My leg took a bruising and the muffler burned a hole in my jeans, but I'll live."

"Go down to the house and get your mother to take a look." Macho Man was still the concerned dad.

"Nah. Let me give you a hand first. We have to get the bulls back in the pen."

It's funny that we bovines generally know when we have overstepped the mark. That's not saying the same thing as we won't overstep it again. Any animal that feels itself threatened will always react. The trouble was, from that day on, U-U's temperament would always be on red-alert. He would always be dangerous to humans. It was WhizKid who saved the day. As soon as he had received his punishment from that two by four, U-U had gone over to join the dominant bull, probably because that was where he felt most secure. WhizKid looked around, decided that this was all too boring, and headed back to his pen of his own volition, taking U-U along with him.

Not long after that, U-U was consigned to follow Beelzebub to the ABHR, the Aged Bulls' Heavenly Retreat, up there in the sky. Jim Carberry had no intention of keeping around any animal that had nearly killed one of his family members, even if that member of the family had been a bit too pushy. The bull would likely always be a threat.

Subsequent events proved Jim Carberry right. U-U did not go without drama. When Mike and his dad went to load him, U-U made it abundantly obvious that no human being was about to make him go anywhere, and that any human being who might have other ideas could look forward to taking an unscheduled flying lesson.

"Let's run him out with Whiz," said Mike, who had learned his lesson and had no further desire to tangle with the animal.

"Of course," responded his father. "Why didn't we do that in the first place?"

They had not done it because of the residual fear that humans have when they are dealing with both the unpredictable and the dangerous. WhizKid simply walked out of the gate when he realized this was what they wanted. U-U followed him up the alley and into the holding pen, and the gate clanged shut behind them. Dad Carberry had very sensibly put out a couple of piles of chop on the ground and that was enough to settle both animals down, not that WhizKid needed any settling down.

Slowly, the elder Carberry reopened the gate and offered WhizKid, who was nearest to him, his own exclusive and bigger bucket of chop. U-U moved nervously but wasn't about to stop eating from his pile. WhizKid ambled back out and gratefully accepted his very own portion of grain, while Dad Carberry locked the gate behind him. From there, it was easy enough to run a still heads-up U-U into the trailer and slam the door. U-U was history!

Chapter Thirteen — The Rites Of Spring

As I'm sure I told you somewhere before, a cow's life is all about reproduction. One could be forgiven for thinking the same thing about *Genus Humanitas,* the way some of *that* species carry on. So, in a sense, the only good cow is a productive cow, which means a pregnant cow, or a cow raising a calf and trying to get pregnant at the same time. Humans should be thankful that their own productivity is not defined by the level of their reproduction, thankful that their fecundity is not critical to the economy, and thankful that breeding is part of the voluntary service sector, so to speak! For us cows, though, it comes down to being pregnant or soliciting pregnancy. It is a fact that cows raising twins often miss getting rebred when they are supposed to, which to me sounds fair enough because during the year I had the twins, I was doing double duty. Logical, right? You would think so, but because *Homo sapiens* has this ongoing obsession with numbers, those numbers only seem to refer to the here and now. So, any cow without a calf is getting "a free ride", no matter if she had a whole darn litter the previous year. This is why when the annual preg-testing came around, dear Katie held her breath for me. What if I was "open"? What if her dad insisted on shipping me out because I was not in calf? Sure, I looked as big as an over-endowed hippo; but pronounced her know-all father, "You never can tell." The visiting vet was apprised of my history and advised to go slow and be absolutely sure of his conclusion because I was "Katie's favourite cow". A more sinister statement was added. "There are no passengers on the Carberry spread," said Dad, playing God.

To their great surprise, I made it all so easy for them. Expecting the worst after my uncooperative behaviour of last year, I was held back to the last. When the time came, I walked straight into the squeeze voluntarily. I stood there passively, well not so much passively as anxiously, while they jabbed at me with their syringes, and shivered, unmoving, as they poured their stinking anti-parasite chemical all down my back. As humans in their hubris might say, "I took it all like a man". Even with the preg-testing, even when the sanitized man in his sanitized suit stuck his sanitized hand up where sun and moon don't shine, I maintained my composure.

"She's good," pronounced the vet.

"She is today," said Big Dad, throwing his first bouquet ever my way.

"No, I mean she's bred," said the vet. "Reasonably early too, I'd say." Katie, on hand because it was Saturday, was overjoyed.

"Thank you, oh thank you," she gushed. Hell, anybody would have thought he was the one responsible for my condition, the way she carried on. "And thank you so much, Lucky, for behaving yourself," she added, rubbing me on the neck.

What did they all know anyway, this hodge-podge collection of *Genius Humanitas*? Did they think a sex life was fulfilling only for humanoids? Could a plain old cow like me not enjoy a bit of fun too? My oh my, there was no possible way I could have been open, not after that hot Bossa Nova I had danced with WhizKid last summer. Hot? It had been positively volcanic! Whoever had named that stud WhizKid had sure called it right; he scored a touchdown every time.

I could blabber on some more about winter and how hoar frost is so pretty and snow so poetic. All I will say is that this specific winter spared us all of the trials of the previous one. We wandered through it at our leisure, and soon enough found ourselves back in the crisp renewal of spring. More yet, like too much of humanity, I could babble on about the wonders of weather, generally, and send you one of those postcards that say "Wish you were here!" Truth is, I don't wish you were anywhere because I wasn't into lucky pennies and wishing wells, and all that human superstitious toiletry. By this stage in my life, I was a seasoned foot soldier. I knew what was likely to come, even roughly when, and I was perfectly satisfied with that. Actually, I have to say I was pretty contented. Pucky and I were a duet. Our babies were sired by the same gorgeous hunk of sirloin. In essence, we were both pedigree Shorthorn, and both of us were committed to "sprog", to deliver our babies at much the same time. What more could I wish for?

We never expected to deliver on the same day though; she in the morning, and I in the evening. She gave birth to a magnificent little roan heifer of about eighty pounds, a heifer so instantly full of life. Thankfully, Katie abandoned her silly practice of rhyming names and called her Sparky. For a few minutes, Katie even considered rejoining 4H so she and the calf could go on the show trail, but the darker memories of the past, of Mike having to send Humpy off to slaughter, soon disillusioned her. She could not bear to watch her companions once again raise a calf as a pet only to consign it to the butchers. No, our Katie was very much a pro-lifer; Pucky was testament to that.

Maybe, just maybe, Sparky's arrival was a message to me to get on with it. By suppertime, it was all done and I was a proud mama to a hundred pound bull calf. I didn't know it then, but for the Carberrys and me it was potentially the start of a new dynasty. Carberry X-Treme was pedigreed enough to be retained for consideration as a breeding bull. Foolishly, Dad Carberry discussed this line of thinking with Katie. That was it; that was enough, of course. He, we, they had to keep X-Treme as a bull and see how he turned out. Ah, the best laid plans of cows and men.

"We'll chance it," was how Dad Carberry summed it up.

"We shall," echoed his daughter, now quite the "farmerette".

Animals growing up are really not much different to humans growing up. As a mother, sometimes you look at your offspring and conclude they are not growing at all, even though they might be eating enough to feed a horse to obesity. You look again a couple of days later, and you find yourself wondering where *that* shape came from, all those gangly limbs if you're a human, all those angular bones if you're a bovine. Animals, human and bovine, basically describe a shape in advance and then grow into it. In late adolescence, for example, Katie was all legs and arms, and so flat I would have said she should never have been kept back to be a mother. Suddenly the day came, and it struck me how all that had changed. She was beautiful, eye-catching enough to catch the unabashed interest of many a would-be suitor trolling by. Likewise with both X-Treme and Sparky; both started out cute as could be, until a zigzag growth pattern established itself. Zig, and us mothers were left wondering how we could ever have conceived such clumsiness; zag, and we marveled aloud at such body confirmation. Zig again, and our offspring had most of the attributes of a donkey. Zag again, and they were so stylish they could be the stars of their own reality show.

Except, except that Carberry X-Treme had one unsavoury habit. As a parent, you've got to hate it when one of your progeny develops an unsettling habit that you seem incapable of curing. For instance, some males of *Genius Humanitas* sweat profusely, and no amount of deodorant, disinfectant, bleach, or paint thinner can cover it up. Or they go around picking their noses. With my X-Treme, he took to suckling from the back, which was okay until he bunted as lots of calves do. The trouble was, when he bunted, he got a full load of excreta on the head. I mean, I was only bovine, what could *I* do? There were days when he looked so awful, I considered renaming him Carberry Shithead or Carberry X-Creted Upon.

We cows pay no attention to dates. Why would we? Calendars are for people who have nothing better to do with their lives than measure time. Suffice to say, then, the first of June meant nothing to us, but to

Jim Carberry, time being money and all that, the first of June was the day he liked to officially stop feeding us. All cows should be on pasture by then, because the grass should be green and growing faster than the cows could eat it. It wasn't that we took issue with that idea. Let me assure you, when you have been consuming nothing but dry matter for the preceding six months, some of it mildewed and moldy because it had been harvested in less than pristine conditions, you'd do anything for a bite of green grass. Just think for a minute how humans might react if all of their food came in powdered or packaged form…Whoa! For a lot of them, maybe it does as so many of them prostrate themselves before their electronic altars with a TV dinner at arm's length. But goggle-box groupies apart, many humans would find themselves breaking out, as we tended to break out, looking for something more freshly natural to eat. Some cows were better at breaking out than others. Maybe Pucky and I were just a little too rotund, but our old friend Whippet could insinuate herself through any barbwire fence and feast on the greener grass on the other side. She was also very devious about it, never staying long enough to attract the attention of the government. And she always went through when none of us were watching, so we never figured out how she did it. Oh, she was a smart one! Except for the day she actually broke two strands of the boundary fence that was supposed to separate us from King Charolais and his pansy-white purebreds. That day, we all went through and got a good two hour's feeding at Charolais Dude's expense before the man himself stumbled upon our presence, which in turn led to a wonderfully un-choreographed flip-out, freak-out routine. Essentially, he was very unhappy and he showed it, especially when he contrived to soil his going-to-town get-up with flecks of fresh manure and mud. I could see how he got it on his shiny new cowboy boots. But right up there on his felt gray Stetson? Come on! He was madder yet when he discovered the solar fencer was not switched on. How was he to know that the young Mister Carberry had been sent up the evening before to do just that, switch the fencer on? But he had been accompanied by a hot young filly clinging to him ever more tightly with every bump they rode over on the quad. Quite understandably, he had forgotten what he was supposed to do, given all that rubbing and shaking, and instead he had done his part in the age-old enactment of the rites of spring. Ah, but he did return with jaunty step and a smile that would have told all, had anyone seen it.

So Mister Charolais set to and fixed the fence right then and there, and turned the fencer on before heading down to the Carberry yard to register a formal protest. Faith came to the door to greet him. She knew it might be bad the second she saw his manure-compromised attire. No, he wasn't coming in for a coffee, he said, but the Carberry "critters" had broken the fence and had chewed up "half the pasture" he was saving for his replacement heifers. He had had to put the Carberry critters back in and fix the goldarn fence, and by the way he had turned on that there fancy solar fencer that had not been on... He took a breather at this point, allowing Faith her only chance to speak.

"But, but the fencer was already on." Faith could look quite formidable when she was bordering on the indignant. "We sent Mike up there...last evening... to, er, to turn it on...and well...maybe he somehow forgot..." The deceleration of her sentence suggested that perhaps she was recalling her own misspent youth, or that she had suddenly realized how her teenaged son might have been misspending his. She was wondering how to placate her neighbor when Charolais Charlie started in again.

"Say, you have a young Shorthorn bull calf in there. If you folks ever want to sell him, call. You hear me? He's a real dandy. He'd do a good job on my commercials, I'm thinking. Anyhow, I gotta be going, but I wanted you to know about them fence-crawlers of yours."

Faith's "I'm so sorry," fell on Charlie's dust, so to speak. She had not planned on telling her husband about the breakout because she knew exactly how he would react. He would go ballistic, forgetting that he was a bit of a fence-crawler himself at Mike's age. Faith knew her husband well, naturally; she had lived with the elder Carberry male all those years. She had a good understanding of hot blood and hormones, and she could see that Mike was his father's son in that regard. But she had to tell him of Charlie's offer to buy the calf.

"What? You mean a devout Charolais man offered to buy one of our scrub bulls! You sure he wasn't joking? That'd be like a Catholic priest offering to conduct a Hindu prayer meeting. Are you sure?"

"Never more sure," said Faith earnestly.

"Well now, that's a real turn-up for the book. Wow, he's a real hotshot cattleman so we must be doing something right. But hold on a second, when was he over here looking at our cattle?"

"Er, well, er, he..."

"Mike forgot to turn the fence on the other night, didn't he?" Mothers tend to forget that fathers might just know their sons as well as they do.

"Right," said Faith hesitantly. "But don't go..."

"Ballistic? Oh don't you worry about that. But he won't go forgetting again."

How could he? That weekend, Mike came home with the same eye-filling young filly of two nights ago, and the whole family sat down for that obligatory four o'clock cup of tea around the kitchen table. Mike and his pert young damsel were sitting together of course.

"Say, my boy," said Dad Carberry in much too hearty a voice, "what exactly did you turn on in the field the other evening, because it sure as hell wasn't the solar fence."

The ensuing silence as profound as it was, the deepening crimson on the poor girl's face, and the boy's gasping for air all amounted to an unspoken summary of the story itself, thankfully without the visual prompting. Finally, a muttered "we forgot" directed into the bowels of Mike's teacup was all that needed to be said. Thank heaven Judge Carberry rested his case, even if his teenage daughter either couldn't or wouldn't.

"What were you guys *doing* up there?" she asked with all the wrong emphasis. What did she want, playback in slow motion? She was studiously ignored.

If I had known Charolais Man was ready to haggle over my kid, well not kid—a kid is a baby goat—over my calf, I would have put the run on him right there and then. But I was back into enjoying summer and discovering that the grass on my side of the fence was just as green and just as tasty as the grass over there in Charolais Charlie's pasture field. You might be wondering at this juncture where WhizKid had got to in all of this. He was with us. Why had he not gone a little further and claimed some Charolais mamas for himself? Simple. Quite a few of us were cycling at the time, and we retained his undivided attention.

The one other unforgettable thing about that summer was the incident at the dugout. Now, I hate dugouts. I hate everything about them. But for many of us on Alberta farms, they are the only source of water. It doesn't matter when or how you drink that water, however, it always tastes of mud and dung. The banks usually crumble away, so many cows just walk into the water, and *voila*, a fresh stirring of the mud and dung we're already drinking. It doesn't matter, either, whether we're talking summer or winter; dugouts are dangerous. In winter, they ice over. Whole herds have been known to gather on the ice looking for water, only to crash through and drown because the ice could not support the weight. I, myself, went through the ice once; I just made it out before my legs froze solid. Never again did I venture out onto a dugout in winter. I ate the snow and I licked the ice. Summer can be no better, especially after a bout of heavy rain. One of the Gelbvieh moms named Fleabag was to find this out the hard way. Fleabag? Katie of course, who else? Kate named her Carberry Fleabag because she was all too obviously the hostess to a range of parasites, evidenced within a week of her arrival in

December; nothing that a good dose of that stinking chemical pour-on couldn't fix, mind you.

Summer and winter may vary in consistency with temperature and precipitation. The more rain, the more heat, the "goopier" the mud becomes. Now put a thirteen to fourteen hundred pound cow onto that mud and locomotion either forwards or backwards becomes a real trial of strength. If you happen to be one of those mamas like Fleabag who gives her all to her calf, then strength is definitely something in short supply. Fleabag ventured two steps too far into the dugout in her quest for cleaner water, and the scene was set. She drank her fill, yes, but when it came to reversing out, she realized she was stuck. Her instant panic made it worse, far worse. Feverish efforts to turn or go back only succeeded in miring her more. She was up to the belly, high-centered with no firm ground beneath her feet, and there she stayed from noon until early evening. She would have died there had it not been for dear Kate.

When Katie got home from school that day, she decided to go for a spin on the quad, and where best to go but up to the pasture to tell us her latest. We were down at the dugout at the time, so she putt-putted down the hill, switched off some distance away so we would not get spooked, and came on over. At first her eyes made no sense of the haggard-looking creature up to her belly in the water, but it soon dawned on her that this was a cow in deep distress. That quad went from its usual putt-putting to full scream ahead as Katie bolted for home to call out the ERT squad, the Emergency Response Team. Thank God all the members of the team happened to be at home. Thank God that Faith had once again hung the sling up on its hook after she had found it hanging on a fence last fall, right where her husband had forgotten it after pulling a stuck haybine out of a mud hole. The Carberry Four came up by various means of transport; Katie on the quad, Faith in the tractor, and the two men in the pickup.

Fleabag hadn't gone anywhere. She was inert, exhausted, and getting colder by the minute. The question now was how best to proceed. Even if they could have gotten close, they would never have been able to thread that sling around her belly or feet or anything in that mud. The only alternative was to try and run the sling under her head and around her chest and then to attach each end loop to a chain running to the tractor drawbar. The hope was that they could pull her out backwards.

Even when Mike went to put the sling around the poor beast, he nearly got impossibly mired himself. But he made it. Now it was the parents' turn to put on a show that had the two younger Carberrys almost spellbound: "The Mom and Pop Show." Mom and Dad were working together in perfect harmony with Faith driving the tractor and Jim on the ground ensuring everything was the way it should be. Oh how proud those two kids were, especially of their mother who handled the tractor with all the finesse of an expert. Faith knew exactly what her director on the ground wanted; her director on the ground knew she would do exactly what he wanted. First they had to take up the strain very slowly, then strain a bit more as they checked the cow, then more strain, check again, and then go for it if the cow was not over the top in distress. And so it all came about. Katie had to look away at "the second strain", certain that the cow would crumple up in its own skin. She looked back just in time to see the full force of the tractor pulling the cow out of the mud on her butt. And there she lay, legs numb from the cold, as much from the mud as from the water. So Mike and Katie went down to the yard for hot water and they washed her down as best they could while she munched on the fresh hay they had brought with them. By then, darkness had descended but at least it wasn't desperately cold.

"Leave her be," said Faith. "She'll be fine. In the morning she'll be up on her feet with the rest of them."

She was.

Chapter Fourteen

Deal Or No Deal!

And so on we went through the summer to the Homecoming, that day when the main herd arrived back home from pasture, arrived into the field where we were pasturing. Right then, there were new grounds for war and the defense of our territory. Once again we had to bang heads together to remind ourselves who was who in the herd's royalty stakes, so when "the outsiders" were unloaded, there was the usual pushing and jostling between two herds that had been apart for some time. Remember Dread, Dreadnought, she of the huge horns? Well, when she disembarked from her trailer, I was the first cow she saw that was not from her own herd, and for some inexplicable reason she decided I needed to be taught a lesson. She must have suddenly decided she was Joan of Arc or something, and that I was a pagan or a wandering heathen in dire need of conversion. Okay, so we had never exactly been friends but we had always gotten along, if largely by staying out of each other's way. Not any more. She didn't look that good either; she was gaunt, had lost a lot of weight, more than any calf could have sucked out of her. The moment she singled me out the way she did, I knew this was about far more than deciding who was who in our bovine ranking; this was "a cow gone rogue".

As soon as she stepped out of that trailer, she took a few seconds to get her bearings, saw me standing there defying any of the newcomers to take me on, and presto, she obliged. This was not simply about territory or hierarchy. This was full-blown, offensive war. My problem was that it was Dread who had the WMD, the Weapons of Massive Destruction, horns that tapered so sharply they could easily have been categorized as armor piercing. She had always shown herself unafraid to use this arsenal, but up until this moment, she had never sought to kill any opponent outright. She was also tall, much taller than me, and that gave her a significant height advantage. But with my weight and a lower center of gravity, I was more compact and likely a lot quicker on my feet. Still, she was Goliath with his club, and I was David minus the slingshot.

Snorting like a wounded bison, she came for me, one horn missing my eye by mere centimeters but piercing my neck enough to draw blood, lots of it. The truck driver and Dad Carberry looked on in astonishment, but what could they do? The only way they might have separated us was with a tractor armed with a front-end loader, but on foot, no way. I was on my own, but I had forgotten my soul mate and ally, my very own Pucky. While the other cows stood back to watch the outcome of what was clearly a blood feud, Pucky launched herself from their midst. She was built like I was. If Dreadnought was a battleship, then Pucky was a cruiser, sleek and fast. Head down, she plowed into the area close to Dread's front shoulder and put her down, and down she stayed, her front leg broken. We turned away then, Pucky and I, and left the scene of the crime, warm blood flowing down my neck from the flesh wound. Fortunately, the two hominids had seen it all and knew that this time Dread had played her final hand. As they approached to check her out, she bellowed at them with the anger of insanity, actually succeeding at getting to her feet to continue her defiance. Her left front leg hung down grotesquely, as if announcing to the world that it was her time to move on.

"She's finished," said trucker Stewart, tersely. "She's plumb psycho, too, if you ask me. You're going to have to put her down."

"I don't have a gun," said Jim Carberry. "Or I'd drop her right now, right where she's standing."

"I'll go home and get mine. You can't leave her like this." Stewart was always the ultimate team player.

"Would you? I'd sure appreciate it. I'll go down and get the tractor so we can tow her out of here once we're done. I'm gonna have the vet come out and do a BSE test." Dad Carberry was not happy. Beyond that, he was very puzzled as to why Dread had suddenly flipped out. They would soon know. They did a BSE test anyway, and it came back negative, and at least that was a relief, but I'm running ahead of the story.

In the meantime, the kids got home from school. Their father recounted what had happened. Katie was instantly certain that I, her bovine soul sister, was undoubtedly dying and that she should be on hand to administer last rites. It was all her father could do to calm her down and wait for Stewart. Who knew what Dread might attempt if Katie went up there by herself? Cows can move on three legs, not well it is true, and Dread probably not at all, but who knew what killer instinct had taken residence in her brain? Stewart returned soon after the heavy-duty family discussion. Both kids wanted to be on hand to see for themselves. Not out of some sort of morbid curiosity or macabre voyeurism, but just to see how this sort of thing was done. Lessons in farm life have to include death if they are to be meaningfully comprehensive, and death often involves putting a timely end to needless suffering. Stewart was the perfect teacher, no histrionics just plain business.

"Picture an imaginary cross from one horn to the eye on the opposite side. That's where you put the bullet, that's where you aim for," he told them prior to leaving the yard. "That's all there is to know."

When they got back up to the pasture, Dread was right where they had left her, and she was evidently waiting for their return if her heads-up defiance was anything to go by. They could see that she was in great pain, the kids shuddering at the sight of her front leg hanging so hideously. They could also not miss how she was seething internally from some unspecified rage. The single shot rang out and it was all over. Dread dropped with a great thumping sound, her death so completely instantaneous she never knew what took her. Surprisingly to Stewart, there was no squeamishness or undue drama on the part of the Carberry kids, just resignation. For Mike, the deed was done, necessarily, and he gave it no more thought. Katie was far more of a philosopher. For her, the whole incident had been more unsettling, not in a maudlin sort of way but in a philosophical one. In one split second she had witnessed an entire existence blown away with one shot. The whole identity that made up the story of that existence had been obliterated as though it had never been, and all that was left was a cadaver. Oh sure, the story's ending would be told over and over, how this darn cow went completely freaky and so on. It also bothered her greatly that a cow could "go off its rocker" like that.

"Why?" she was compelled to ask Stewart. "Why would a cow suddenly do what she did?"

"Well, let's see now," said Stewart the farmer, the rancher, the trucker, a man who had handled thousands of cows in his time and in so doing had come across many "anomalies" such as this one. He walked over to the cow, and with Mike's help pried her mouth wide open. There, at the back of the lower jaw was a massive, festering abscess that had not just centered on a tooth but had invaded the entire back of the throat.

"Poor old gal had a giant toothache," said Stewart. "Being squashed up in the trailer like that must've triggered a 'kill 'em all' instinct when she got out and saw a bunch of cows she wasn't used to. That's my story anyhow, and I'm sticking to it."

"Makes good sense," commented Mike.

"I'm going over to the other cows," said Katie. "I need to see how badly Lucky got hurt."

"I'll come with you," said Stewart. "Mike, here's your dad coming up the road with the tractor. Can you give him a hand to get her out of here?"

Kate was, in her own way, grateful that Stewart elected to go with her.

She wasn't scared of me, or anything; she was more scared of what she might see. With Stewart around, she would have a second and seasoned opinion to count on. As for his volunteering to join her, that elevated him into someone special in her eyes, far more than a simple acquaintance that merely did the Carberry's trucking. By rights he could have gone off about his business, but instead he took the time to ensure there was full closure to an incident triggered by work he had been doing for the family.

It was funny. When I saw Katie approaching in the company of a man I had only ever seen at distance, I didn't run. I sensed that his concern for me was on the same level as Katie's, so I let them come right up and check me over. Katie had brought a can of antiseptic spray with her in hopes that all I had was a superficial wound that looked worse than it was, and which was indeed the case.

"You don't need to lose any sleep over her," said a relieved Stewart. "She won't come to any harm and that spray will stop the flies pestering her too much. But boy oh boy, that's sure a dandy bull calf she's got. You need to hang onto him as a bull. Holy smokes he sure is a well-built young fellah!"

That was it! That statement of Stewart's was the clincher, the final argument in the case for keeping my boy back as a breeding bull. But the advice he went on to offer was even more important. "Now don't you folks go do what so many of us dumb farmers do and keep him on the farm. You gotta send him off to some kind of bull-testing facility, that's really the only way to find out what you have got. Now don't let that old dad of yours talk you out of it!"

Actually, Stewart had got it wrong. Dad Carberry knew he had to do it right, if he did it at all. He accepted that he himself had no idea how to raise a bull for optimum results. He could also see what a pain it would be to raise a single yearling bull at home; it would have to have its own designated pen and it would be lonely. As for what you should feed an over-wintering bull prospect, he really had no concept. Did you feed it an extra skiff or two of hay? Did you give it an extra couple of buckets of grain a day because it still had a long way to grow? At a recognized bull-testing station, the bull would be in a homogenous group and would receive a balanced diet calculated specifically for a bull that age, appropriate bedding, a health program that left nothing to chance, and, joy of joys, a ream of numbers and statistics that would have made any human happy. Of course, such numbers as these can be a double-edged sword. If your bull performs at the bottom of the group, then all sorts of folks are going to read how poorly Carberry X-Treme is performing, but that was a risk Dad Carberry knew they had to take. And so the big decision was made.

At weaning time, X-Treme got to stay with me a couple of extra days in a pen all to ourselves, while the rest of the calves went their designated ways. But let me expand on that.

What is the matter with us cows, at least with the majority of us? I have a theory that might explain it. We cows are too easily distracted; a bit like humans, really. We are especially distracted by food, as are many humans. I have to admit, you put a tub of grain chop before us, and our bovine brains slip quietly into "park". The difference between humans and us, though, is we are not unsettled by as wide a range of distractions as *Genius Humanitas*. All sorts of things distract human beings. They see a "celeb" trying to keep all the prominent bits of her body inside a garment designed to display them, and they are mesmerized. What about automobiles? Put a Maserati or a Ferrari in front of any human male and he goes so gaga; heck, he wouldn't even know it if he was run over by a train. They, humans, are bad with food, too, which is why they start to salivate at the thought of any dessert with an exotic name: "Cheesecake à la Froppingnon" or "Mousse à la Tortuosité". So don't go telling me how stupid we bovines are to be caught once again at weaning time with a serving of chop! From here, we were quickly corralled, and just as quickly separated from our offspring, except, hey what's this now. X-Treme and I were held together. That Sparky, too, was held back with a few other heifers as replacements didn't make it any easier for Pucky, especially when she could see me still with my baby in our own special pen. Well, hardly "baby", he was just as big as me. Ten days we were together in that pen—ten whole days in an attempt to get X-Treme at least a little habituated to boarding house food. Then one morning, the Carberry trailer rattled up to the loading chute, my boy was loaded up, and I was sent back to the field with the rest of the cowherd. That was it, the end, and another betrayal by *Homo Treacheritorious*.

Of course I was not privy to the unfolding adventures of Carberry X-Treme, **Sire:** Greenacres WhizKid, **Dam:** Gronkspread Lucky, but they do deserve mention. Carberry X-Treme was shipped to the Cattleland bull-testing facilities in Strathmore, Alberta, there to join a group of twenty-five young Shorthorn bull calves belonging to an array of established breeders across the province. He was by no means the biggest—not the thinnest or the fattest—and not the only roan in colour, either, but he looked just as good as any of them. He looked better, thought Kate who had skipped a day's school to make sure her X-Treme got the right treatment and all due respect. To her surprise and delight, the person in charge of bull testing was a lady, a lovely lady with the unlikely name of Mrs. Ann Leapyear. She didn't look anything like the cowboy Katie had expected, and there was no wad of "Copenhagen snoose" folded in below her bottom lip. Hell, she didn't even wear a cowboy hat! She was just a plain, down-home lady in jeans who clearly knew her job and her bulls.

"That's one fine young bull you've got there," she told Katie, when Dad Carberry explained he was just the driver and Kate was the owner. "He's set to go places. I can see that already."

Kate took to Mrs. Leapyear instantly, and knew that X-Treme was going to be in the best possible hands over the next six months because she and he had made Mrs. Leapyear into a friend.

Six months X-Treme was there, six whole months. The testing itself took only one hundred and twelve days, but it spewed out a bunch of numbers that told Miss Katie Carberry that she was sitting on a real winner: a bull with all the right stuff. Indeed, his numbers told such a story of quality and vigor that he was awarded a plaque for "the top gaining bull of the year" in the Shorthorn pen; correction, Katie S. Carberry was awarded the plaque for her top gaining bull, Carberry X-Treme. Now given that humans are sometimes no better than cows at knowing their places in the hierarchy, the award to Katie S. Carberry put quite a few noses out of joint among the premier breeders in the province.

"Who *is* this Miss Katie S. Carberry?" one miffed cowpoke matron sniffed at Mrs. Leapyear. "My Muddy Creek Poet of Xanadu Rock was the best bull in there. Even you must have known that?" She didn't wait for Mrs. Leapyear's response because she knew the old adage that truth hurts. "Does this Miss Katie S. Carberry run a big operation or what? My husband and I have never heard of her, and I thought I knew everybody worth knowing in this business."

Another sour grape of failed country gentleman lineage wanted to know how some upstart kid's 4H bull calf could possibly turn out to be top gainer in a professional bull test. "You guys must have made a mighty big mistake, I'm thinking."

"Go take a look at the bull for yourself, or take a second look if you've seen him before," Mrs. Leapyear responded, oh so demurely. "He tells his own story, so no, we didn't make any mistake."

You can almost guess how it went from there. The Carberrys brought X-Treme home with a view to using him on some of the herd. Three days after he was back on home turf and safely installed in his own pen, the phone rang at about noon on a Tuesday.

"Hello. I'm looking to talk to er, hold on, I have it here, to a Miss Kate S. Carberry," said a man's voice, betraying an age somewhere in the fifties or sixties.

"I'm afraid she's not here right now. She's in school. Can I help you? This is her mother, Faith Carberry."

"In school, you say. Oh, oh, you mean she's off at college, right?"

"No, in high school. She's in Grade Ten."

"Oh. Oh, well, maybe you can tell me who I talk to about the bull she had in Strathmore on test."

This was where Mama Carberry spoiled it some. "Well, I guess you can have a word with my husband. Hold on please." She handed the phone to her mate.

"Hello, Jim Carberry here."

"Hi, Jim. My name is Richard Saunders-Wagstaff and I live out here just south of Trochu. Say, I'm wondering how much you're willing to take for that bull of yours, the one that was on test at Strathmore, the one named Carberry X-Treme."

"Well, to be perfectly honest, he's not mine," Jim said with a hint of smugness. He knew how it went. The fellow probably hoped to buy the bull for next to nothing because it came from an unknown breeder. "The bull belongs to my daughter. What might you offer for him?" He was quite certain this was the question that would put an end to what was surely a fruitless conversation.

"Well, you know how tough it is these days ..."

Here it comes, Dad Carberry was thinking, an offer of fifteen hundred delivered.

"... blah, blah, blah ... but I could offer you, er your daughter three for him. There's something about him I really like ... blah, blah, good confirmation ... blah, blah ... sound feet, like the way he stands ..."

Dad's mouth was like that of a goldfish in its bowl, he kept pursing his lips as if waiting to be fed. "Three?" he said, trying to come to grips with what he was hearing. "Like three thousand?"

"Three thousand", said the voice. "Best I can do."

Jim Carberry was in shock. He himself had never paid more than two thousand for a bull, and this fellow was offering *three!* "Well, that er, that sounds like a reasonable offer to me," he said. "I shall talk it over with my daughter when she gets home because it's her decision. I should tell you, though, that a neighbor wanted the right of first refusal on him. We would have to see what he would offer first."

"Fair enough," said the voice. "Just don't go and sell him out from underneath me. I want a fair shot at him." He spelled out his name and number and Dad Carberry said they would contact him by the weekend.

If Dad Carberry could hardly believe his ears, his daughter was beyond belief. Wow, three thousand dollars! Wow, three thousand dollars was a small fortune—enough to buy the fancy mountain bike she always wanted, and a new snowboard, and a VCR, and…

"That'll sure help pay your way through nursing school," said her mother, pouring water on any further grandiose ideas. But still, to Katie this was really something new, an entry into the world of high finance and Wall Street. Wow, this gave real meaning to what they did for a living. They called Charolais Charlie who came over right away.

"Three and a half," he said when he had looked X-Treme over. "It's my one and only offer, good for twenty-four hours. If the other fellah beats that, take it. Remember, my offer is good for twenty-four hours. Take it or leave it." Doing business with him was like doing business with a machine gun, Dad Carberry was thinking. "If the other fellah doesn't take him, call me, you hear," this directed at Katie as if she was a Grade Six retard.

"Why does he have to talk like a machine gun?" said Katie, as he stomped off to his truck and headed home.

Dad Carberry insisted that his daughter be the one to call Mr. Saunders-Wagstaff. The phone rang twice before a mellifluous voice said hello.

"Hi. I'm Katie Carberry and I'm phoning because I hear you are interested in my Shorthorn bull. Actually we had not planned on selling him, but now we're not sure. My neighbor just offered me three thousand seven hundred dollars."

"Three seven, you say? Three seven. Humph. Tell you what, I'll offer you four even, how's that?"

"Four thousand?" Katie's voice almost squeaked in excitement. "Hold on a minute, I'll just ask my dad."

"Your bull, you're selling him or keeping him," said Hands-Off Carberry.

"You just got a deal Mr. er, what did you say your name is?" Katie never even heard his response she was so excited.

So, too, did my own sweet Kate get herself a deal. But then again, it wasn't every day that an animal like my Carberry X-Treme came along.

The flipside of the story turned out to be darker but very interesting. If my Kate had sold my X-Treme to Charolais Charlie, he would likely not have made it beyond the first breeding season. More about that in a minute!

Chapter Fifteen

Try The Word "Moronic"

Actually, this is as good a time as any to fill you in about what happened over at Charolais Charlie's place, and it's a darn good story too. Come to think of it, us being close neighbors and all, it could just as easily have happened on our place, and one of us could have wound up in the mortuary. Remember how I told you that humans rely on numbers to tell them pretty near everything—clocks to tell the time, calendars to tell them how old they are, that sort of thing? When that calendar announces a certain date in the fall, every intrepid Nimrod within 200 miles of the West Edmonton Mall drops his TV remote, climbs into his pickup and heads out to kill a Whitetail or a "Muley" or anything else that foolishly traverses the crosshairs of his scope. The calendar tells them that what they are now doing is legal if they do it between this date and that date. Outside of these specified dates, however, hunting is illegal. It's amazing the power of numbers—even on a calendar!

Another thing about *Genus Humanitas*: in the same way that spiders can spin the most intricate of webs, so human society can come up with various forms of government all of which spin their own webs of rules and regulations, and of course a fair number of these apply to hunting. Humans seem to think that the level of regulation is in some way a measure of how civilized they are, and their laws supposedly demonstrate how enlightened they have become and how far from the apes they have evolved. But little do they realize so many of their laws actually show how *under*developed they are. Why do they need all these rules in the first place if they are so wise? Of course there are many among them who believe that rules are only made to be broken, while others would happily obey any rule as long as it doesn't apply to them. Maybe that is why, as a species, *Genius Humanitas* has involved itself in so many conflicts, more than any other species on the planet. But, anyway ...

So at a certain time of year, hunting brings forth not only an array of legitimate hunters who respect the law but also a crop of hotshots for whom any land that doesn't boast a shopping mall or a Tim Horton's is their rightful hunting terrain. Such as these would never consider cruising the country roads in anything less than a truck that announces to the world that it is "4X4 Off Road" and that it can see at night with a set of spotlights sufficient to light up the whole of downtown Red Deer at two in the morning. These are the "Roadkill Boys"; the guys with the latest in bargain bin shades and discount binoculars, dudes in camo pants naturalized in the interests of safety by vests in orange technicolour so they won't shoot each other if they are parted in the heat of a chase. These are the same dudes who never ask permission to hunt on a person's land until they are actually caught there, and once caught don't have the class to ask forgiveness. These are the same guys that can barely tell the difference between a Doberman and a Collie—let alone the difference between a live Whitetail and a burlap sack hanging in a tree—until they have holed it a minimum of three times and a maximum of 21. They are the ones who never think a missed shot might carry a mile or more and drop some poor old bovine gal grazing peacefully in her pasture on the next hill. To them, if you are black, brown, magenta, or scarlet with yellow polka dots and you show up in their scope, it wouldn't make any difference.

When the Carberrys passed over Charolais Charlie's offer to buy my X-Treme, he had to look elsewhere for a commercial bull, settling for a much cheaper Simmental at one of the spring auctions. But with bulls, most of the time you pay for what you get; something even I could have told him, if he had asked me. By the time Charlie got his bull home, he was kicking himself for not doing better. Oh well, he'd use the bull for the season and sell him in the fall. Only he had not got around to it when the hunting season opened. Actually, it did not just open, it broke out like World War Two, if all the rifle shots going off in the area were anything to go by.

Too often, hunting is about power unthinking, about men extending their dominion over Mother Nature rather than working with her to share her bounty. For some, harvesting the wild game meat was at best incidental, at worst an unnecessary chore. Young men who think this way need far more than a mandatory firearms course; they should take a course on the philosophy of nature so that they learn to respect life, and especially a life they might be preparing to sacrifice. In this regard, I'm glad for myself and for my offspring that we always had proprietors who were more than mere cattle barons; they were genuine custodians of the sanctity of life. Most of them, anyway. Most of the time.

One more time shots rang out, this time to the south. The first week of the hunting season was always the worst. This was the time when so many of the city boys would escape from their concrete jungles. Anywhere where there were lots of trees and no houses, "hey, that's the boonies, man!" For them, two hours from their city's outermost mall was "far enough into the sticks" to bag whatever they had decided on hunting. All they needed to do then was drive up and down rural gravel roads, looking for a creature to shoot, often draw or no draw. The longer it took to come upon the "right" deer, the more impatient they became, the itchier the trigger finger, the stronger the urge to shoot at, well, just about anything. The two characters driving around the Carberry place that day were the pick of the crop: so much in image, so little in substance.

Image and humans, now there's a can of worms! So many people get hooked on image, only to find themselves trapped by it. A suit is not a suit unless it is an Armani. A watch is not a watch unless it is a Rolex. You know how it all goes. Now these two young bucks were all image. Not quite Ernest Hemingway on safari (neither of them had ever heard of Hemingway), they were nonetheless a compilation of all they had seen in the movies, of all the straight shooters featured in the hunting magazines they had ever looked at, all spiced with a vivid imagination free to roam wherever it pleased. To give that macho image a little bit of extra bang for the buck, both were drawing beers from a Character Pack tucked behind the seat. By the time they had made it across from Charolais Charlie's, they had stopped to draw beer number five and to lament their lousy luck. It was early evening, a couple of hours before the sun had done its work, when that magnificent Whitetail buck stepped tentatively onto the road about 200 yards ahead. The dominant one, the one who wore the name Butch because he saw himself as a dominant alpha male (excusable in his present company), immediately reached for his rifle and started to squeeze himself slowly out of the truck.

"You, you can't shoot him on the road," his buddy Ernie whispered hoarsely.

"Who says?"

"But, but it's against the law. If, if we were to get caught..."

"Who's gonna catch us then, eh?" Butch grinned as he exited.

Poor old Ern was compelled to swig another mouthful of beer to control his panic and to allay his wimpishness.

Just as Butch sighted his trophy and was on the point of squeezing the trigger, the buck spooked and bolted across the road and off into the bush alongside the pasture. Butch let go a string of words he had never learned in school when Charolais Charlie's truck crested the hill before them. It was he who had spooked the Whitetail. Ern had never seen his partner in crime move so quickly. In seconds, the gun was gone, the door was shut, and they were moving along the road. Ernie had to confess he didn't like the way Charlie looked them over as he passed by. Butch just laughed and then launched into a tirade of his own.

"Son of a bitch! We could'a had him!" He shouted. "We could'a had him. Tell you what. We'll drive a mile down the road and come back. That buck hasn't gone that far."

Ernie was instantly in a funk. "What if that guy comes back? He sure gave us the evil eye as he went by. Maybe the buck ran onto his land." Ernie had to state the case for the wimps.

"Nah, he won't come back. Besides, how many vehicles we seen down here anyhow, eh? One truck in four hours? Nah, that old fart has gone home for supper. We'll go turn around by the river and head back up here. That'll give the old bastard time to show up, if that's what he's gonna do, right? Right?"

"I guess."

"You sure are some kind of a wuss, you know. Suck on another beer. You'll get over it."

Ern took the advice, and man, it sure helped; his apprehension quickly dissipated in a beery mind-fog. As Butch had suggested, they turned around down by the river and nosed their way back up the hill, stopping on the way to study the patch of brush into which the Whitetail buck had disappeared. There were a couple or three cows about, but they were happily grazing and paid no attention.

"There! There he is, the son of a bitch." Butch suddenly whispered fiercely.

"Where? Where? I can't see nuthin'," responded a sidekick who regretted drinking so much beer now that he was seeing double.

Butch did not bother to reply. In an instant, he was out of the truck with his rifle. Using the hood as a rest, he fired at his target in the brush. It went down.

"Got him! Got the sucker! Man, that was some shot, eh? He went straight down." Ern didn't move, didn't even react. "C'mon man, what are you waitin' on? Let's go get him and get the hell outa here."

Ern fell out more than he got out of the truck, and together the two men hot-footed it through the fence and into the brush where Butch had bagged his buck, Butch's imagination already picturing a six-point rack on his living room wall. But for all his manliness, and for all of Ernie's drinking, Butch was slower than his companion. Not seasoned in any form of physical locomotion, Butch never went anywhere without wheels so he lagged behind, panting like a spent billy goat. It was poor Ernie who got there first, and what he saw caused him to recoil in horror. The animal his partner had shot was not the buck at all; it was a great big brown and white cow, and it was deader than a stone. He decided not to say anything. His friend could see for himself.

"Oh shit!" said Butch when he arrived, wheezing for breath. "Oh shit and double shit! Why didn't you tell me it was a cow, eh? Oh shit. We'd better get outa here fast." They turned towards their truck. There, parked right behind it, was the same truck that had passed them a while back; the one that had spooked the buck in the first place. The rancher was sitting there, watching them through his binoculars.

"You leave the talking to me, eh?" said Butch on the way back. "I'll cook up some story or other. Just make sure you shut the hell up, eh?" That was fine by Ernie, now trailing his friend in a blind panic. The rancher let them get right up the fence before he spoke.

"Say boys, nice evenin' for a bit of hunting?"

"Sure is," Butch regretted that statement as soon as he said it because it implied that hunting was what they were doing. Thank God he had left his rifle in the truck.

"Say, I've got me a bit of a problem," said the voice a little too hard-edged for Ernie's liking. "See, I don't remember givin' you boys permission to hunt on my land."

"So who says we're huntin', eh?" Butch's aggression was always a mite quicker than his brain.

"I says." The rancher responded flatly.

"Oh yeah? So why aren't we carrying guns if we're out hunting like you say?" Butch could bluster his way out of this, just as he had always blustered his way out of everything. "Where are the guns, dude?"

"In your truck, wise guy," said the rancher coolly.

"Oh, so now I'm a wise guy, eh?" Four, five, six beers, nobody had been counting, a dulled brain, and a penchant to get into a fight all started to render the situation into a disaster.

"Well, we thought we saw a fox going into a den over there in them bushes," said Ern in a desperate attempt to save his skin. He had always been good at creative writing at school. "So we went through the fence to check it out. I've never seen a fox before."

"A fox, you say? Hmm, did this fox have any horns on his head by any chance? Like a six-point rack?"

"What in hell are you talkin' about?" Butch felt compelled to take charge.

"That buck you boys went after. That's what I'm talking about. The Whitetail buck you just shot on my land."

"We never shot no buck on your land. Like my buddy just said, we just went to see if the fox we saw had a den in that brush. That's all. Now we're real sorry we were on your precious land, but I'm afraid we gotta go now. We gotta be back in Red Deer in an hour." Butch began climbing through the fence when the rancher's next words stopped him in his tracks.

"Sorry boys, but you are not going no place," the rancher smiled almost benignly. "See, one of the Fish and Wildlife boys is on the way to check you out. Should be here any minute. My advice to you is to stay put until he gets here."

"I ain't stayin' put for nobody," Butch snorted. "Not for you, not for some dude from Wildlife, not for nobody. C'mon Ern. Time to get outa here." Butch climbed through the fence.

"Oh shit! Oh shit!" muttered Ern, climbing through the fence after his mate. Ern was not very happy.

"Ugh, the truck's locked. You got the keys, Ern?" Butch was checking through his pockets as he put the question.

"No, we never locked it, remember?"

Only then did it dawn on them. Butch turned slowly to face the rancher.

"Yep, don't you worry. I got the keys," he nodded. "Thought I'd better lock up that high-powered rifle you left on the front seat. You shouldn't leave a gun like that unattended in an unlocked vehicle, on a deserted rural road like this one, while you go off looking for foxes. Hell, you boys should know that."

"Look, Mister." Butch was now verging on a new, more cooperative attitude but it had been a little too long in coming. "Let's all just climb down from our perches and settle this thing without a hassle. We're real sorry we were on your land without your permission. Now, if you'll just give me the keys to my truck, we'll get outa here and we'll never come back, I promise you." It was too little and much too late. Even Ern could see that after his five, or was it six or seven, beers. The rancher's next statement, pitched as flatly as it was, put Ernie in a blue funk.

"Here's what we're gonna do. We'll all take ourselves a little walk over to that clump of brush and see if we can see that fox. We might even find its den because I happen to know there is a fox that hangs around here. By that time, the fellah from Fish and Wildlife should be here."

"Hold on Mister, we are not goin' anywhere. Nowhere. You're gonna give me my keys right now, and we'll head outa here." Butch had to make this one last offensive in hopes of getting out of what was a bad situation that was steadily getting worse. "If you refuse to give me my keys, I'll call up the cops on my cell and tell them you have stolen my truck."

"Oh, you go right ahead big fellah! Might as well phone the fire department and the ambulance, too, so we can all have a party."

"You, you know what? If you don't wanna give me my keys, then we're gonna have to come..." Butch never got to finish his sentence because a dark green pickup with the Alberta Fish and Wildlife logo on the door pulled up behind the rancher. A big lanky man stepped out.

"Hey there, Charlie. Howdy boys. So Charlie, you got a problem you say?"

"Sure do, Chuck. I'd like for you and me and the boys to go take a look for a fox that ran off into that patch of scrub, over there." Charlie winked at Chuck, a wink "the boys" never saw.

What could "the boys" do but go along? They could not make a run for it; that cunning old rancher had the keys to their truck. So Butch did the best that Butch could think of in the circumstances.

"I just want you guys to know," he said, as he lagged behind the Wildlife officer and the rancher, "I just want you guys to know that I wasn't the one who killed the cow. We found it in there, and that's the truth, isn't that so Ernie?" Ernie grunted for he knew that Butch would only add to their woes. There he was, basically admitting to the landowner that he had killed one of his cows, something the rancher did not know yet but was about to find out within the next 20 or so paces.

As soon as they came upon the dead animal, Charlie said, "This ain't my cow, son."

"Oh that's bloody great," said Butch, "because I guess I hit it by mistake."

"No, my friend, this ain't my cow," Charlie repeated. "It's my bull."

"Oh God," said Ernie speaking for the first time in quite a while. "I told you! I told you not to go after that damn buck! I told you we should go home. I frikkin told you…"

"You're both under arrest," said the Wildlife Officer. "I think it would be best if both of you came back to my truck, and we'll do all the stuff we have to do. I'm afraid you'll be facing a number of charges. You have the right…" And the rest was history. But, and this of course is why I took the time to tell you all of this, it wasn't my X-Treme that was lying dead there with a bullet in the skull, yet it could so easily have been him if Charolais Charlie had bought him. And to those of you who like to use the word "bovine" to put somebody down when their brainpower is sadly lacking, try the word "moronic" instead, it's more bovine-neutral.

Chapter Sixteen

Package Deal!

So much for deals and bulls and the human moronic/criminal elements, the onset of winter signaled the end of an almost non-existent fall. Even the trees that year didn't seem to get around to shedding their leaves. The snow started to fly way too soon and it snowed too often. And like an uninvited mother-in-law, it stayed around until the spring. Like seasons do every year, this one also boasted its own identity. Not bone-chilling cold but cold enough; it was the constant trudging in the snow that became our particular cross to bear, and beneath it all was the ice, treacherous and slippery. Keeping our footing was paramount, but even so the herd had suffered two abortions by Christmas; both were the result of slips on ice. Fourteen hundred pounds of living cow does not crash with any more dignity and any less drama than a little old lady, I can tell you. In fact, fourteen hundred pounds of living cow crashes like a brick outhouse going down in an 8.7 earthquake. With a body that large, muscles and ligaments stretch, tear and bruise, and that Great Arbiter of Life, Mother Nature, decrees who shall live and who shall pass on—even if they might never even have opened their eyes on this tumultuous world. This is why there was always a gang of coyotes hanging around, for they too had a designated role, to scavenge on what Mother Nature had seen fit to discard. Since the Carberrys seemed to resent their presence so greatly and took a shot at them whenever they had a mind, those coyotes became wily beasts; wily enough to stay beyond the range of men too sluggish to pursue them on foot.

Preg-testing and vaccination came due in the middle of a cold snap. The day was sunny, yes, but not warm, so the vaccine had to be kept from freezing in Mama Carberry's little, old Toyota. Nonetheless, I'm sure you don't want to hear me go on about how cold exacerbates pain; believe me, it does, for me at any rate. This year I was not singled out and held over to the end. Instead, I was run through with the main herd, so I managed to muscle my way into the second batch to go down Happy Alley and into the squeeze. I shivered but behaved with stiff upper lip when Katie herself did the vaccinating. She did it so expertly that I didn't even realize she had injected me twice. She would thump me on the neck a number of times with her fist before the needle went in, so the actual dirty deed was done before I got too much reason to protest. Preg-testing was worse because the metal probe was so darn cold, but at least it was quicker than the old low-tech route where the vet went on a fishing expedition with a gloved hand.

"She's early," he said. "Early or big. Probably both."

No surprise to me, I knew whom I had been hanging around with. Katie was happy. I knew that much because she told me. Better yet, she mentioned that Pucky was right there with me. Not that I knew *exactly* what she was talking about, but that doesn't always matter when you're bonding with someone you worship. The message was clear.

"Oh, and you know what, Lucky? Next year Sparky will be right there with you," Katie added, so proud that three generations of Lucky were going to calve in the same year on her behalf. And talking of generations, Carberry X-Treme would be sowing his seed somewhere out there in the big wide world, and the Lucky dynasty would be growing by leaps and bounds. So what did that make me? I was the equivalent of a high-priced professional hockey player with a score of plus 22 in my career. There they are again, those infernal statistics! Oh well, at least they won't trade me like I'm a lump of hockey meat; I'm far too valuable to the Carberry Bovine Sabers!

By the time calving season began, it was still snowing: not a huge amount, just a skiff or two a day. Mercifully, the Carberrys had brought in plenty of barley straw so we were as comfortable as we could be, even with the snow. Furthermore, the vet was correct. Pucky and I were clearly going to be early; the Carberrys could see that in the build-up of milk in our udders. We were put into the barn together, sharing the same pen because there was not much "room in the inn" with a heifer occupying the adjoining pen. How was Kate to know that putting the two of us together would turn out to be a big mistake? Inexperience? Probably, but then experience is only the knowledge gained from previous mistakes and put to use in such a way as to prevent them occurring again.

I'll say it now, and I'll say it like it is. I can be, and could always be, an absolute bitch! Not a doggy bitch, but a real cow—the most ornery female my species has ever known! Now if you want to take offense here because I'm using unparliamentary language, it's your choice, and I know how you humans are so big on choice. Take a pill or something. I can also say that I came by my "bitch syndrome" honestly. Remember my mother? Eat, sleep and defecate; that was my mom. Oh, and give the Gronks a run for their money. Having a calf was an incidental inconvenience built into her cycle of eating, sleeping and defecating. Human males often find themselves counseled that if they insist on committing to marriage, they need to take a hard look at their prospective mother-in-law to figure out how their valentine will turn out over the long term. That's why the mother-in-law joke is so overworked among humans. Certainly as I grew older, I became intolerant and more set in my ways. And this particular year, I didn't feel that hyped up about calving. I knew what was coming, yes, but I didn't feel like doing it. So when Pucky calved first—somewhere around midnight—and delivered a nice roan bull calf. I got it into my head that I could save myself a whole lot of trouble if I took over her calf and adopted it as my own. Sort of a "package deal" you might say. This didn't just happen; I had to fight for it. After all, Pucky was from the same stock as me, and she wasn't about to donate her calf to what I thought was a worthy cause. It was all a bit unfortunate because our relationship was never quite the same again. I had always been one to decide what I wanted, and I wanted that calf and I wanted him *now,* and nobody—not Pucky, not Katie, not even Dad Carberry armed with a piece of two by four—was going to stop me taking it. By the time I had finished my business with Pucky, she was standing in the one corner nursing her bruised ribs, and I was standing in the other nursing her calf. No labour pains for me, not this year, no painful contractions measurable on the Richter scale, no pain and no muss, just an instant baby like it just came in the mail. Or so I thought—so secure was I in my arrogance, my "bitchiness".

Shirley Jackson

It all changed at four o'clock in the morning when Kate stumbled into the barn, dear sweet, half-asleep Kate who had slept through her alarm set for two o'clock. Dear little-less-than-sweet Kate who was already mad at herself because in her mind she had screwed up by not getting up when she had wanted.

"Oh Lucky, you've got yourself a new baby," she cooed when she saw me with the calf, standing guard over it as if he were a trophy. "Are you going to let me take a look to see what you've got?"

I must have had a shred of morality left in my soul because my guilty conscience kicked in. A conscience is truly an obstacle to the conduct of efficient criminal business, and so it was in this instance. When Katie made a move to come my way, I made the move to tell my own *alter ego* that such an idea should not be entertained. Katie evidently got the message loud and clear but couldn't understand why I would be sending such a message to her of all people. She took another step forward and I became downright menacing. No doubt about it, I could not be trusted.

She turned for the door, and that was when she saw the afterbirth hanging from Pucky. That stopped her in her tracks. She spun around just in time to see my tail end, and instantly she knew what had happened. I threatened her again, almost taunted her to come and take my calf, if she dared. Then I made it clear that she should get out while the going was good. That was my mistake. I should have known that Katie was too much like me; she was simply not one to be intimidated. It worried me though that she had still kept her composure, how methodically she went about the business of making doubly sure she had read what had happened correctly. Then she drew in a deep breath, as if she had come to a final decision. Now, she knew that bringing Dad Carberry into the act would likely make matters worse. I'd have him hanging in the rafters in a second. Hell, in the mood I was in, I was tempted to put Katie up there, too. I watched her take a pitchfork from its place on the wall, and without a second glance at me, she quietly opened the gate into the adjoining pen and closed it behind her. Good, she had lost interest in me. Talking softly to the heifer, she escorted her out of the exit door into the holding pen outside. She came back in, closed the door, walked back through the now empty pen, opened the gate and came on through without ever once looking my way. Well fine, she could ignore me all she liked. What did I care, just as long as she left me alone with the calf. She disappeared out of the barn and into the night.

She was back two minutes later with a half-bucket of chop. Pucky looked up hopefully, poor old cowering Pucky, and went on disposing of her afterbirth. Katie motioned to me to come for some chop. Oh that devious little woman, she knew my weak points! I took a couple of hesitant steps towards her. She moved toward the open gate into the other pen, pitchfork back in hand. Nice try, but I wasn't about to fall for that! I turned to see if the calf was still there. He was. She called and I turned, and she tried again. Once more I was very tempted, even taking four steps forward only to see Kate and bucket make for the empty pen. I was having none of it! None! Did she really think I was that stupid! That old saying from "The Bovine Book of Unlikely Wisdom" comes to mind when I explain what happened next: "When you think you are the best at playing the role of champion bitch, beware; there is always another who can play the role better than you".

Katie lost patience. She had every right to lose her patience in the circumstances: she was tired, she had school in the morning, she had exams the following week, and here I was—her favourite cow no less—playing the role of ultimate bitch. This was not some United Nations sponsored peacekeeping mission, where as commander on the ground she was required to phone Head Office New York, read Dad Carberry in bed, to get permission to change the R.O.E, the Rules of Engagement, before she could take the offensive. She just did it.

I asked for war; she would give me war. I knew as soon as I saw that frown come over her face, that hard glint take over the eyes, that steely resolve stiffen the body, I knew that I was in for a fight I would not likely win. It wasn't this understanding that so unnerved me though; it was the sound, yes, *the sound*. It was a shriek, really—the wail of the banshee. (**Banshee :** "female spirit of Gaelic folklore believed to presage death in the family…"). That sound, that eerie, extraterrestrial howling indubitably presaged some awful demise as Katie launched herself straight at me, the tines of the pitchfork aimed at my heart. Bravery in the face of the enemy is one thing, especially when it is inspired by the knowledge that you are fighting for a good cause. But when you have a guilty conscience as I did, and when your enemy is your only human friend suddenly transformed into a howling creature from another world, there is no shame in retreat—even disordered retreat. I ran. I bolted for that open pen as if all the hordes of "Hannibal the Hun" were on my tail, and I took refuge in the farthest corner, trembling in my terror. The horrible screeching ceased immediately. Kate closed the gate, and then told me in no uncertain terms *NEVER, EVER* to threaten her again.

She then went over to my, er Pucky's, calf. Now Pucky had been just as traumatized as me by Katie's weird behaviour. She stood in her corner and watched, her maternal instincts urging her forward, her instinct for plain old survival holding her back. The calf was a good-sized bull calf. Nice and cozy, he had no desire to move; after all, he had had his first full meal from me. Katie was insistent and forced him to his feet. She walked him over to his mother, talking to her softly all the way. She picked up a chunk of afterbirth and rubbed it on the baby's back to reestablish the right scent and threw a handful of chop on his back that Pucky would lick off. Pucky needed no further persuasion. She knew that calf was hers, knew that it was now hers to keep, and started to mother him at once.

That was when Katie took me totally by surprise. I thought she would head off to bed in a huff, but no. She came back into my pen, put down a small plastic feeder, and poured a third of a bucket of chop into it; her way of burying the hatchet, I supposed. I was not about to go anywhere near her though, not yet, not with the noise of that crazed banshee still ringing in my ears. She left without more ado. I waited until I knew she was bodily out of the building before I dared to touch that grain. It certainly had the desired effect because I soon settled down, my heart resuming its normal rhythm.

I looked through the gate. I knew I shouldn't have because I knew that what I would see would make me wild; there was Pucky's calf, happily sucking from his mother. I lunged at the gate. I would show her a thing or two, you bet I would. I slammed into the gate. It rattled but did not move, the noise only serving to irritate me further. I butted it with my head; it butted back, steel on bone. Okay, so I would go back and have another mouthful of chop and think about things. And another, and another. I looked up, feeling a little better when the first contraction hit me, almost dropped me on top of the pot. I staggered back to my corner. The second contraction, stronger yet, compelled me to lie down and get on with it.

One hour later, and after the greatest pain I had ever endured in my life, I was done—exhausted, but done. Here again is where young Katie stepped back into my life with her knack of knowing when she was most needed. I was so fatigued, I did not have the strength to get to my feet; I just lay there. What I did not know—could not have known—was that a portion of the birth sack still covered my baby's head and nose and preventing it breathing. Nature demanded that I get up and lick it off, but then nature had left me totally out of gas.

For some reason, call it human intuition, Katie had been unable to get back to sleep. She did some schoolwork for a while, and then something called her back to the barn. She did not so much come in as burst in, and spotted the crisis in an instant. She almost dove through the gate and ripped that incredibly tough piece of membrane from the calf's face. It blinked. She grabbed a piece of straw and stuck it unceremoniously up his nose, and his lungs immediately took up the challenge. She stuck it in his ear and that stimulated him further. She got him up, and he responded with a pathetic little moo. Pathetic though it was, it brought me unsteadily to my feet. I was nervous. Would Katie suddenly transform herself into a Gaelic witch and attack? She talked softly to me, and dragged the calf close by so that I might sniff it. One sniff was enough to energize me, and I took charge of a bull calf that was the splitting image of X-Treme, only bigger, chunkier. He responded with gusto, and Katie knew then that she could retreat in triumph; she had saved the day.

"You have to stop doing things like that on your own!" Dad Carberry was quite incensed when she told him the story.

"What? And have Lucky put you through the gate or up in the rafters?" she retorted a little too truthfully.

Dad Carberry could acknowledge the truth. Nevertheless, he would never have been able to forgive himself if something ever happened to his only daughter, especially if it was because of a stupid old cow. "All the same, at least let one of us know you're out there." He finished somewhat lamely.

"I know my limits and I know my Lucky," said Katie.

Too true, too bloody true, Dad was thinking. "But then again, think how the rest of the family would feel if something bad happened to you out there, and we didn't know about it. Your actions would be giving three family members a burden they would have to carry for the rest of their lives. That's the bottom line."

"Dad, you always make sense. You're right. I promise I'll let you know next time."

In the meantime, Katie's lively imagination didn't let her down. She named my big monster Carberry Yeti, for this was the year of the Y. Pucky's bull was named Carberry Yogi, and if you had put the pair side by side, they were near as big as each other.

Now don't ever think a cow cannot feel remorse. I felt bad and Katie knew it. But Katie was right back to being Katie, despite all the drama. For Pucky, it was a bit more complicated. Katie had the advantage of being able to rationalize my erratic behaviour and put it down to a mixed-up cocktail of hormones out of control, misplaced maternal instincts, and the bloody-mindedness of my nature. So it took time for Pucky to come back into the fold, so to speak. It took time for her to trust me. Our old friendship was rekindled over time, but it was less of a relationship and more the mutual enjoyment of each other's company. Like the old metaphor, our friendship was a priceless vase that had been dropped and restored, but the cracks would always be there. But such is life, no?

Finally the weather broke and gave us what we all craved, warmth and bright sunshine that led us seamlessly into summer. This particular summer was uneventful: no stinky skunks, no spiny porcupines, no dramas in muddied dugouts, no breakouts into Charolais Charlie's pastures. The one thing I could see, though, was that as much my Yeti was exploding into something truly magnificent, so Katie was metamorphosing from a gangly, teenaged, high school basketball star, into a stunning specimen of *Genus Humanitas* in her own right. Yet to my mind, the beauty of her caring personality and her open mind more than matched the beauty of her physical appearance. I could have been labeled as the bitch from hell to be avoided at all costs because of my antics at calving time, but they were never held against me. Katie treated me as she had always treated me, and as the righteous shall always be rewarded, so Katie was rewarded with the deal that came out of her approach. You see, because I was never afraid of my mentor, so too did my Yeti become habituated to her. He was a gentle soul, and so he too became enamoured of Katie. This in turn led Yogi to be drawn in, and together their temperaments became so mellow, they could be approached by almost anyone. And so they were, oh so they were—much to Katie's surprise and delight.

Chapter Seventeen — The Dog Days Of Summer

It was the tail-end of summer when the phone sounded one evening in the Carberry household. "Answer it, Kate," said a mother weary of fielding calls for the second most popular woman in the world after Paris Hilton.

You know, it's funny, but we cows get to wonder how talking has become an addiction for such large numbers of humanity. Can't they do without the sound of their own voices or what? One would think that with the advent of all their shiny new technology, cell phones and all that stuff, they would have a whole lot of profound things to say. For myself, I have concluded that people are no different to monkeys; when monkeys get excited, they chatter furiously among themselves. Now it seems obvious to me that if people insist on being in constant verbal contact with other people, then behaviourally they have to be the kith and kin of monkeys. We cows have often seen our Kate take a call on her Nokia cell phone. When it sounds, all too often her eyes go vacant and she is instantly distracted. If by chance it turns out to be the latest flavour of the week, well, she wouldn't even know it if her hair were on fire!

But back to my story. When the phone rang that summer evening, Katie took the call on the landline. "Hello," she said tentatively in her neutral voice reserved for those people whose names she did not recognize on caller ID.

"Oh hello and good evening," a clipped male voice responded. "I'm looking for Miss er Katie Carberry, please."

"This is Katie Carberry."

"Ah, Miss Carberry. This is Richard Saunders-Wagstaff, out to the east. How are you doing?"

"*Who? Who* did you say you are? Do I *know* you?" Kate was caught completely flat-footed and she knew it. Her usual good manners were entirely missing.

"Well, I hope you do remember me. You see, I'm the fellah who bought your Carberry X-Treme bull last year. The name is Richard Saunders-Wagstaff."

"Oh. Oh, I am so sorry, Mister Wagstaff." Kate actually felt a lot more than plain old sorrow. She felt both foolish and poor, as if all her gold was about to crumble into dust. "Oh, er how did X-Treme make out for you?" At least she had the courage to pose the question when she expected the worst.

"Well, that's actually why I am calling you," said the voice enigmatically.

Katie was on the verge of panic now. "He, he didn't work out for you, did he?" The man was probably looking for some money back, or...

"Oh he worked out for us, my dear, don't you worry about that. He's the best darn bull I've had in thirty years. He's a real dandy."

"Oh!" Katie's heart went from pounding with fear to bursting with pride.

"No. What I am wondering is whether you have any more bulls where he came from. Like, you still have his sire, WhizKid, do you not?"

"Oh yes, we still have WhizKid. And, actually the mother of X-Treme and her daughter, too, both have bull calves, so we have two bulls we kept back for sale."

"Well now, that sure is good news," said the voice. "What I'm wondering is whether I could drive out to your place one day and take a look at them."

"But they're still calves." Katie's business mind had not quite caught up with her excitement.

"Oh, I realize that. What I'm thinking is that my wife and I will take a drive out your way, and make a quick stop at your place to take a look at the calves, if that would work for you?"

"Oh for sure. That's not a problem. Both of them are on the home place anyway."

"So how do these two young bulls compare to X-Treme when he was their age, would you say?"

"Pretty much identical because they're both from the same line." Katie's rising confidence was making her into a business tycoon by the second. "But I had planned on putting them into the same Strathmore bull test as we used for X-Treme so they get the right nutrition over winter."

"Yes, of course. I wouldn't expect you to do anything else. What I'm looking for is once again the right of first refusal if they turn out good. I'm assuming you'll be looking at the same kind of money as you got for X-Treme, right?"

"Right," Katie agreed immediately without even having given it a thought.

"So if I may phone you next week and set up a time, would that work?"

"For sure," Katie responded, trying desperately to keep a lid on her excitement.

Wow! Just wow! What if she could sell Yeti for another four thousand dollars? Wow, she would be downright rich: four thousand smackeroos, even if they had to sit in her bank account like the first four thousand she got for Carberry X-Treme.

And so it transpired. The man picked a Friday because Kate had no school that day. He arrived in an aristocratic pickup—a silver Lincoln Navigator—accompanied by a blue-rinse wife as aristocratic as the pickup, a wife with the obligatory aquiline nose that looked down from a great height upon the unwashed masses. As could be expected, she did not deign to alight from the vehicle in order to consort with lesser beings and other assorted mammals.

"Methinks plain old green cow shit doesn't mix with noble blue blood!" was how Dad Carberry was to put it later. But he of the hyphenated name, oh he waxed ecstatic, indicating that he was very impressed. We cows could have cared less about him and his waxing; we were enjoying a visit with our Katie.

"Temperament, you see, Jim. It's all about temperament." When you have a prospective buyer full in flight, you endeavor to listen closely, as did Dad Carberry. "It's like picking yourself a wife, you know. Now me, I picked one with all the goods except for an easy-going temperament and look where it got me. I do the farming and her ladyship instructs me on how to do it, where to do it, when to do it."

"Humph," said Dad Carberry, not wishing to take on an additional role of marriage counselor to the rich and not so famous.

"Anyway, you just take a look at them two bull calves. Peas in a pod, they are, peas in a pod. Now me, I see real potential there, real potential. Young lady," he called out to Katie who left us to hear the jury's verdict. "Young lady, I would like first dibs on both of those young fellahs, right? If I decide when the time comes that I don't need 'em or want 'em, then I'll let you know. But I want first refusal on both, you hear me? You go ahead and put 'em in the bull test, and we'll see how they do. And let me tell you right here and now, they're both gonna do fine. But don't you dare go selling either one of them out from underneath me, okay?"

"Okay," said Katie, with a grin that threatened to make even Garfield at his happiest look sour.

"Would you like to come down to the house with your wife for a coffee?" Dad Carberry was compelled to extend their hospitality even to Mrs. Saunders-Wagstaff, president of Sometown's "Ladies of the Empire".

"I would love to, but I'm afraid I shall have to take a rain check. As you can see, my bride is not much the visiting kind." He added as if in explanation, "She is more English than the English, you see. She claims to be related to Lord Portleman of Crabtree Castle, as if that means a whole lot to this dumb Canuck."

That was it, the full extent of the visit and the deal.

"Don't go counting your chickens before they hatch, my dear," Dad Carberry counseled his daughter as soon as the visitors had left. "A bull can get sick or hurt or he may not even pan out the way we thought, no matter how good he looked as a calf. You never can tell."

It was wise counsel in view of the subsequent events with the dogs, and the disaster that could so easily have happened to Yeti. You should know that as a rule, cows and dogs don't mix. Leave working cow dogs out of this. I'm talking the pet variety. Some people see dogs as some kind of fashion accessory, while others see them as an extension of their identity. Look around or go to a dog show, and I'm quite sure you'll see what I mean. The exquisitely coiffed Pomeranian will quite likely have an exquisitely coiffed duchess in tow. The man with the ugly pit bull will boast the same facial features as his dog, and the regular Joe with the Doberman tends to lift his leg on things much as his pet does. Canines are fine with us bovines as long as they are disciplined, on the end of a short leash or chain, tied to an immovable object, or just plain dead. Yes, I am putting it rather bluntly, but if you'd ever been hunted by a pack of yowling dogs, then you'll know at once what I am talking about and why I say what I say.

Our spot of trouble goes back to the proliferation of acreages in the country; those five to seven acre plots subdivided from viable farms so that the new owners can set about constructing their dream palaces with a view of the mountains, unspoiled by the addition of the neighbors' underwear flapping on a clothesline next door. Cash-strapped farmers held hostage by hostile economics sold off such plots to pretend country folk—the ones who saw themselves astride a piebald horse, behind a white plank fence singing "yippee-yi-yo" to the imaginary dogies.

To be perfectly honest, many of these types would do far better to head back to the towns and cities they hailed from because they have no idea how to conduct themselves in a rural setting. We watched them constantly fly by in their gigantic, goggle-eyed gas-guzzlers with grilles akin to the jaws of Tyrannosaurus Rex. Do they ever slow down and think that maybe a calf or even a cow may have somehow gotten through the fence? Never! Does it ever occur to them that wire breaks like shit happens? Then if a "doof-doof" occurs(cow slang for "unfavourable and accidental physical contact"), it's always the fault of the dumb animal, if not the dumb farmer who should have been watching his closed-circuit TV to know that one or more of his animals were out. Or better yet, why does he not fit all of his animals with one of those radio-controlled collars, or even hire a designated chaperone…you get the picture!

Yet these same happy, yappy folks have to have their dogs, and because they are going to be living in the wide-open country without the necessity of a "scoop-a-poop" routine, they go for bigger dogs: bigger dog, greater status. Now I'm not against status; status can be a good thing because it makes you feel way more important than you really are. But if you need a Rottweiler or an Irish Wolfhound to massage your ego, then at least keep the beast under some control. Your ego too, for that matter! Their human keepers should consider such pets as being on the same level as a wayward teenaged son with a penchant for the wild side. Do you know where your wayward son is? Right now? At all times? If he's not at home where he is meant to be, then where is he? Could your cuddly little boy be raising merry hell a hill or two to the west, or partying down by the river? Is it possible he has just joined a gang and is roaming the territory out west looking for trouble? Just because you bought an acreage with a view of the mountains, does that give your dog license to travel the dominion from sea to sea to sea?

You know what is coming, don't you? Dogs— four of them already used to running in a pack, one afternoon in broad daylight. The pack leader was one of those great big, shaggy, white Pyreneans that you cannot miss. With him were a Black Lab, a half Rottweiler, and a Heinz-57 mutt, all of whom he had invited to join him for the day from nearby country McMansions. Clearly they were on some kind of mission, the target yet to be determined by their illustrious leader, the Great White One. It was my very own Yeti who triggered the ensuing drama. Always much too curious for his own good, he went to investigate this motley canine crew presuming to cross our pasture. The pack stopped just long enough to give him time to discover fear and legs, and he high-tailed it back towards the sanctity of the herd as fast as he could go. What he instigated was a full-blooded chase, complete with all the "baying of the hounds" you ever wanted to hear. That set us all on the run, which served to get the dogs even more excited, snapping randomly at our heels. All except GWO, Great White One, who had singled out Yeti as an animal he intended to bring down.

We never did see the car stop on the gravel road alongside the field; we never saw anything. We did not see GWO's owner get out of her luxury chariot and begin screaming at GWO. We did not hear her frantic calling to

Snowy to "get on home right this minute", but then Snowy was of no mind to see or hear as he was gaining on Yeti who saved himself by swerving in ahead of me. I stopped abruptly, and there was Snowy right there, right where my left rear hoof could connect where his tiny-brained skull should never have been. They say of a home run in baseball that it is the epitome of perfect timing, a combination of a good eye for the ball and a solid bat. Well, I hit a home run, timed it to perfection and it was all over in the blink of an eye. Well no, that's not quite true. The moment GWO went down, his companions took off for their various villas, and we stopped running. Not for long. Now it was *sound*, not dogs, that put us back on the run: sound, extreme and terrifying, a surreal mix of stirred-up anger and profound distress, all rolled into one. But then again, if the sound was enough to induce flight, the sight that greeted our eyes was enough to arrest it. A spectacle was unfolding before us, something much too good to miss, and we stopped to watch, wide-eyed and breathless.

I would have thought it was a given that city women should never attempt to crawl through barb wire fences when they are burdened with an insecure load beneath a damask business suit of fine cloth. The lady's first sally at the fence left her jacket irretrievably snarled on the barbs. The second foray tore indiscriminately both the tight skirt and the fine silk blouse and caused major variations in the overall shrieking. And then there she was, attempting to stride across our pasture, the metaphorical ship in full sail—well, not quite so full given that some of the rigging had been left behind on the wire. And attempting to stride, because how can any woman stride in high-heeled shoes on soft soil pasture? She was actually picking and sticking her way, when finally the sound indicated that she had had enough. The shoes came off and were flung at the mountains out west in what we presumed to be some kind of pagan ritual. Now bare-footed and armed only with an umbrella, but with a face that was consistently spewing like an active volcano, she thrust herself onward, ready to fend off any bovine offensive from us. Alas, it was all in vain. There lay Snowy as dead as he would ever be: his erstwhile allies and companions long gone. When the woman reached Snowy and discovered the full extent of her tragedy, she simply sat down next to him and howled; let it all loose in one prolonged howling at such gross misfortune. Finally, thankfully, the sound petered out into a sob, at which point she stood up with purpose. It was quite evident that it would have to be her husband who would have to retrieve the body, either him or the farmer! Of course! It was time to pay the farmer a visit because Mister Farmer was damn well going to pay for this one way or another!

Shirley Jackson

Poor Faith Carberry. She was in the middle of a second batch of baking when the doorbell sounded. She rushed to the door. There, standing on the step was one very disheveled and distressed woman. Instantly Faith's mind was forced to grapple with a wide range of signals; the woman was in her late thirties, shoeless, her once smart suit was torn and missing the jacket, and her silk blouse was ripped enough to show rather too much WonderBra. "He's dead!" she wailed. "He's very, very dead! Wah, wah!"

Faith took the woman firmly by the elbow and steered her inside. The aroma of fresh baking was perfect in settling her down. A cup of coffee and a muffin allowed her to regain some composure, to talk more sensibly, and to unburden herself with Faith's prompting.

"Now, who is it that is dead?" asked Faith, wondering if she should be dialing 911.

"Snowy is dead," the woman blurted out to her coffee.

"Oh, Snowy. Now who is Snowy?"

"Snowy is, was, my greatest friend, my soul-mate, and now he's gone."

"That's so sad," said Faith praying that Snowy was not some term of endearment, some precious name she had given her late husband, like "honey" or "pumpkin". "So Snowy is, or rather was…?"

"My dog. My big, white Pyrenean. You people own those cows up on the hill, right?" The fire was coming back into the eyes, and Faith was a little uncertain whether that was a good thing.

"Yes, we own the cows on the hill."

"So it was your cow that killed my dog, my Snowy." The woman was triumphant. "I even know which cow it was, and I want you to have her destroyed."

"I'm sorry. You want me to have one of my cows destroyed? Like shoot her or something?"

"I don't care how you do it, but I want her put down so she doesn't go and kill somebody else's pet."

"But what was your pet doing in our cow pasture in the first place?"

"He was just playing with a few friends when your cow decided to attack and kill him."

"With a few friends, you say? Playing with a few friends?" Faith was so incredulous she had no idea what else to say. Was the dog, was Snowy some kind of surrogate child or what?

"Yes. My dog and three of his friends were playing with your cows when this one brown cow got mad and kicked him in the head, killed him. I saw it all from the road. My husband is going to have something to say about this, let me tell you!"

"Oh, I'm sure he will. But let's back up a little. Let me ask you a couple of very basic questions. Like *who are you?* And where exactly do you live?"

"Oh, we recently moved to the house that used to belong to Robert Hagler. We bought it and renovated it. My name is Lillith McPhee. My husband is Roger McPhee. He's a consultant in the oil patch. He's gonna be real mad, let me tell you. He was very fond of Snowy."

"And what do you do for a living?" Faith was relentless, refusing to be drawn.

"Me? Oh, I work for Matthews and Selby, the lawyers in town. I'm a part-time legal secretary."

"Ah, a legal secretary. So you will understand that for my husband and I, cows are how we make our living? Now we can't just go and destroy one of our cows just because somebody's pooch got kicked in the head while harassing her. That makes no sense. Your dog had no right to be there in the first place. My cow was likely just protecting her calf."

"Look lady, my dog and his buddies were just playing with your cows, not harassing but playing. He always liked to play. But one of your cows just up and killed him, so I think you should do the right thing and euthanize her before she hurts someone else's pet. Or at least you should be willing to compensate us for the loss of our dog."

"Ah, now I see where this is going. This is about money, isn't it? Well Lilly, may I put it as plainly as I can without offending you? We will not be paying compensation for the loss of your dog. I'm very sorry that it happened, but your dog should have been tied up at home and not roaming the countryside in a pack with his buddies, as you call them, bothering other people's livestock."

"How can we tie up a big dog like that for eight hours a day while we are at work?" Lillith really came to life now. "That's one reason we moved to the country, so that we could keep a big dog that we didn't have to tie up all day. We wanted him to have plenty of space to roam. He had a right to space. Why would we tie him up as if we were still living in town? And by the way, I hate being called Lilly."

"Look, Lillian, allow me to make a suggestion. You're a legal secretary, you say. So go ahead and check out the law. I think you'll find that any farmer is within rights to put down any animal that causes distress to his livestock. I guess our cow did the job for us. If you wish us to pay you compensation, then go ahead and file a lawsuit. At that time, you can help identify which of the twenty-five brown cows it was that kicked your dog, and we'll be happy to bring her into the courthouse as a witness to hear her side of the story. One more thing, if you wish to live in the country then learn the ways of the country. Show respect for your rural neighbors and what they do." It was inevitable that the sermon fell on deaf ears.

"Well, the least you could do is show some sympathy," said Lillith reaching for another muffin. "I mean the least you do is pay for my ripped blouse. It's silk you know." She attempted to adjust for excess exposure of WonderBra magenta.

"How on earth did you manage to rip it like that in the first place?" Faith had to ask.

"You try getting through your barb wire fence in a business suit," Lillith snapped back. "My jacket is still hung up on the wire and it's going to damn well stay there. It came from Harrods of London, you know."

"I'm sure it did," Faith responded, now getting tired of all this nonsense. "I'm sorry about your dog, I'm sorry about your silk blouse, I'm sorry about your suit from Harrods of London, even if I do compliment you on your underwear. I'm sorry we shall not be paying you any compensation. You are in the wrong, your dog was in the wrong, and may I respectfully suggest that if you decide on another dog, pet, whatever, make it a Pekinese and keep it under control."

At that, Lillith McPhee rose to full butterball stature. "Hrrumph. You people are going to have to lock horns with Roger. He is not going to be happy that his dog got killed by some redneck cow. You'll be hearing from him very soon, I'm sure." She reached for yet another muffin, spun on her heel, re-hoisted the flap of silk, and sailed off in her monster SUV. Lillith was wrong. The Carberrys never did hear from Roger.

Chapter Eighteen — Just A Cow!

Actually, not only did the McPhees never again contact the Carberrys, they never even took the time to retrieve dear "Snowflake", or whatever his *nom du jour* was, in order to give him the decent burial he deserved. It was left to Dad Carberry to inter him in a pauper's grave, an old coyote den that he modified into a final resting place and canine mausoleum, once he had worked it over with the tractor and front-end loader. Thus did those city folk treat their loyal dumb friend, consigning him to an unknown and unmarked grave through their apparent lack of any concern. Such is the perfidy of those steeped in Mammon!

I could tell you one more time about the heartbreak of weaning and losing our beloved Yogi and Yeti, both trucked off to Strathmore for their bull test, but in the interests of brevity, I'll tell you instead about how Fate dealt me an unkind and ultimately final hand. When the Carberrys served up the grain for us that year in the usual feeders, hidden in the chop was a piece of badly corroded barbwire that had somehow fallen into the mix. You have to understand one salient fact here; when you serve what constitutes a real nice treat to a herd of cows, they are thrown into direct and frantic competition with each other. It's a bun feast, a food fight, an Epicurean struggle among bovines. Imagine a dozen adolescent humans asked to share a giant banana split from a single bowl. Picture the shoving and the jostling, the gluttony and the opportunities for extreme treachery, the urgent vacuuming up of all that good stuff not primarily for the pleasure of savouring every morsel but to consume a greater volume than the neighbor in a shorter time. So too when cows are served with rolled grain, they go for it as if it is to be their last ever meal, as I did on this particular occasion. That was how and when I sucked in that piece of wire, felt it travel down the esophagus all the way into the reticulum or first stomach. Entirely preventable? Absolutely! I could have paused and spat it out, but since it was mixed up in a whole mouthful of chop, I risked losing out on more of the same if I stopped. So I let it go. Some cattle farmers throw a magnet down their cows' throats to prevent what is known as "hardware disease". The magnet attracts stray nails or broken bolts away from the stomach wall where they can do serious damage. The Carberrys had never seen the need to do this. After all, it wasn't as if their chop was full of odds and ends and metal scraps that they knew of. They had never given a thought as to how a bolt might come loose in a combine or how a baler might pick up a scrap of wire, with the items making their way into the food that has been processed for their stock.

Fittingly that fall was beautiful, all russet and poetic, and I was as ugly and irascible as I had ever been. But Katie's attention had been deflected away from her favourite cow whose body should have been restoring itself after raising her annual monster. Katie's final year in high school literally ate up all of her time. It was not that I was neglected; it was simply that I wasn't noticed. My decline was gradual, it was true, for my body fought the inevitable infection every step of the way. The trouble with TR, Traumatic Reticulitis or "Hardware Disease", is that by the time it becomes really obvious, it is often too late. I, for one, didn't need a high-priced veterinarian to announce that nothing could be done for me and "that's a hundred dollars for the consultation, please."

Katie, of course, was the first to notice, and it really set her back. She had come up to our fall pasture for a little visit, a kind of state-of-the-world address, but the words died on her lips the moment she saw me. She had to look again and again as if to convince herself it really was me, then without uttering a word, she spun around and ran back to the house to call her father.

"What's the matter, honey?" Mama Carberry asked, as Kate burst into the house. "You look as though you've just seen a ghost."

"Well that's because I have just seen a ghost," she stammered. "I want you guys to come up with me and take a look at Lucky. I think she might be dying."

Mom and Pop Carberry both came up with Katie, Mike being down in Calgary. Both agreed I was a disaster the moment they saw me. As for myself, I looked at them all with little apparent interest, barely responding to Katie rubbing behind my ear.

"Well, we could give the vet a call but I honestly don't think he's going to tell us much more than what we can see already, and he's only going to charge us good money to tell us that we're too darn late." As always, Dad Carberry did not sugar reality. But at the same time, and mercifully at that, there were no recriminations, no accusations of neglect, for this was a family that carried its loads together.

"Leave us be," said Katie softly. "I'll be down in a few minutes." The others turned away and headed back to the house. This was the first ever time I saw my Kate really cry, not for herself but for both of us. I felt her grief keenly and hung my head even lower. Pucky made her way over and licked my neck a couple of times, as if to show some solidarity, as if to show that she too knew that nothing more could be done. As you might now expect, Katie's biggest concern was how much I was suffering. She couldn't bear to see an animal suffering unnecessarily, and right then and there I knew she was weighing all of her options. Could I be saved or by prolonging my agony was she only assuaging her own guilt at not having discovered my condition earlier?

I was the one to prompt the final decision. I aborted my calf two days later. I was so weak, I just got rid of it and then stumbled away, not ever bothering to look back at the withered fetus I had just expelled. So I never even knew that I would have given birth to a WhizKid heifer in the spring. The Carberrys spotted the evidence on my rump the very next day, but they never did find the fetus. The coyotes had spirited it away that first night; for them as for all the animals of the wild, death meant life and another's survival.

Katie made her final decision within minutes of her parents' announcement that they were going to Edmonton for a long weekend to stay with some old friends. With Mike in Calgary, it was Katie who would have to hold the fort on the farm; feed the cows and do the chores, all the mundane things that had to be done.

The senior Carberrys left on the Friday morning. Katie did the feeding, all the while feeling the sheer weight of her decision crushing down upon her, the desperation lacing her determination with grit and steel. Then she did it, she made the call to the one man whom she knew would come through for her. Stewart the trucker took the call at home just at noon.

"Hello," he answered into the phone.

"Hello! Stewart? I…I need your help", was all Katie could squeeze from her vocal chords.

"Okay," said Stewart evenly. "Do I need my gun?"

"Yes." The answer came back in a whisper.

"Okay. I'll be there in twenty minutes." He hung up and then made a call to cancel his afternoon appointment, telling his customer that he had just been called out on a sudden emergency. There are always sudden emergencies on the farm; people just learn to roll with the punches. With that accomplished, Stewart set off for the Carberry farm.

Kate was there in the yard waiting for him. Once again she had to work hard to get the words out. "Stewart, I need you to put my cow out of her misery. She's, she's very sick, very sick…and I don't want to…to see her suffer any more. Dad and Mom are in Edmonton and Mike's in Calgary," she added in anticipation of his question.

"Show me!" He said simply.

She took him to a wooded copse adjoining a small pasture field, from which she had removed the other cows. I was standing under an old and bent poplar tree waiting. I knew what was coming because I, *we*, had willed it. My special relationship with Katie was a unique form of symbiosis. Within the context of our rustic world, we knew what each of us wanted, what each of us had to have. I knew I had served her beyond all expectations. Among other things, I had been her very own "cash cow", but those days were now over and I knew that Pucky would take over the role.

"Give me one minute alone with her before you do it," said Katie. "Just one minute." Stewart stopped walking and stepped behind a tree while Katie came on alone. She threw herself around my neck and hugged me with all her strength, as if she was trying to will it into me one last time. There was nothing said, nothing, for there was nothing more to say. It was the ultimate communication between two souls acknowledging that this was the parting of the ways. In that instant, we both knew how we were an inextricable part of each other. A profound mutual understanding not penned in some form of epic poetry nor thundered out in some Wagnerian crescendo but unstated in our very own version of ESP, extra-sensory perception. We knew, too, that in its way this was less an ending and more of a hiatus; that somewhere beyond this world, sometime beyond this earthly time, we would be reunited, reunited on an equal footing without Man's dominion over the beasts of the field and the birds of the air. We would be two kindred souls flying together in joyous harmony! That was when she released me, let loose one mighty sob and walked away, walked past Stewart behind his tree, and kept on walking back to the yard looking neither right nor left.

Shirley Jackson

I saw him approach. I saw him and welcomed him with a sense of sublimity. I saw him stop and raise his rifle, unwavering and so conclusive. I even heard the sound of the shot before the crash of the bullet took me and all went black. I felt my body crumple but more than anything I felt the release, a profound release back into the primordial essence from whence comes our being.

Stewart found Katie back at the yard. She came up to him and hugged him lightly. "Thank you," she said almost in a whisper. "Thank you so much."

"Hardware," he said. "No doubt about it. You had no choice. It had to be done. Not a very nice way to die. Are you gonna be okay?"

"*Now* I'm going to be okay," she said. "Now I'm going to be okay. I just couldn't bear to see Lucky suffer like that."

"No," said Stewart. "You made the right decision."

"I'm fine," Katie reiterated. "I just need to be alone for a while to think things through. I'll be fine, I promise you."

"I know. But call me if you need me." Stewart knew then that he was dealing with strength and purpose, so he had no qualms about jumping into his truck and heading on home.

That was not the end of the story, however. Early the next morning, there was a knock at the door. Fortunately Katie had risen early and was having her breakfast. She opened the door to find a young man standing there.

"Are you Katie Carberry?" he asked.

"Yes. Why?"

"Hi. My name is Marty. I've come to bury a cow."

"You what?" said Katie, her mind trying to make sense of what she had just heard.

"I've come to bury the cow. The cow Stewart put down yesterday. Can you show me where she is and where you'd like her buried?"

"But…but how are you going to bury her?" Katie was incredulous.

"How? With my track hoe. My rig is out there on the road."

"But…but what will this cost?"

"Cost? Cost you? Nothing. Me? It'll cost me an hour of my time. This is between me and Stewart. Just show me, and I'll get er done."

So there it was. Lucky in life and lucky in death; buried in my very own grave, tits up, and seven feet under. And on the mound, Katie didn't do all that usual memorial stuff. Not Kate. She planted a tree, a Blue Spruce, and wouldn't you know it grew like the proverbial weed. What did you expect? In life I had been full of the proverbial shit. In death too, apparently!

Even in death I left my mark, both directly with my baby Yeti and indirectly via Pucky and Yogi. They took the one/two in the Shorthorn pen at the Strathmore bull test, thus proving the Carberry X-Treme that went before them was no fluke. Not only did they do the one/two, they did it so convincingly that the Carberrys knew that the $4,000 per animal price tag they were asking was realistic. Even more so when they considered "Yeti's" dam, me, was unfortunately "recently deceased". The Saunders-Wagstaffs asked to meet up with the Carberrys at a Strathmore coffee shop to see "if we can come up with a package deal on the pair", said Mr. Saunders-Wagstaff. Blue Rinse Mama was there too, which was a bit of a surprise given her reluctance to mix with mere mortals.

"Now, let's get down to business. What would you take for the pair of them?" said the husband, adjusting his bifocals to focus on Dad Carberry.

"Beats me," Dad replied. "You'd best ask her," he nodded at Katie. "They're her bulls, after all. And she's the one that needs the bucks for school."

"Very well, young lady. Over to you. What are you looking for in dollars?" The man was almost smug in his attitude. Why would he not be? Dealing with a teenaged business neophyte would be a pushover.

"Well, I was looking for four thousand dollars each because I think that's what they are worth." The teenaged business neophyte served it straight down the line, as clear as any take-it-or-leave-it proposition could be offered.

"Ah. Let me see. Hmm. Well, here's what I'm prepared to do. How about seven thousand for both, seeing as I gave you the price you asked for your very first bull, for Carberry X-Treme. How's that?" He tried to laugh off the low ball. Not that it mattered; it flew straight into the net.

You see, this was where the admiral's wife intervened. "Young lady, what are you planning to do?" Fittingly, the lady had a voice like a foghorn. "With your *life*, I mean?" she boomed. "What are you going to do with *your life?*"

The question almost unsettled Katie, unexpected as it was. "Well, as a matter of fact, I'm going into nursing, specializing in intensive care, I hope. I need the money for my schooling."

"You *hear* that Richard, don't you. The young lass is going to be an intensive care nurse. I knew she had the right stuff."

"Seven three," said the Admiral trying to regain command of the bridge. "That's seven thousand three hundred."

"*Richard!* You just don't *listen* to me, do you?" It was clearly going to be full steam ahead. "The young lady is going to school to be a nurse, Richard."

"Yes dear. Seven five. Final offer. Seven thousand five hundred."

"*Richard!* You are not even trying to listen! She's going to be a nurse. The young lassie is going to be a nurse. She's going to be someone you will probably need in your old age, and pretty soon it will be if you ask me!" She turned to Katie. "Don't worry dear, he will pay what you ask, won't you Rich?"

"Seven six," said Rich, now clearly demoted to the engine room.

"*Richard S-W!* You are going to pay eight thousand, you hear me!" She leaned back in her chair and released a smile that must have been in captivity a mighty long time. "It was *so* nice doing business with you, Miss Carberry. Wasn't it, Rich?"

"So how much was that?" said Rich reaching for his checkbook seconds later.

"Eight thousand," said Katie with a disarming smile.

"Ah, yes, eight thousand," said the man tiredly. "Eight thousand it is."

Later the following spring when Stewart came to do the Carberry trucking, Kate took him to one side. "So how much do I owe you?" she asked.

"Owe me? Owe me for what?" said Stewart, genuinely surprised.

"For doing what you did for my cow," Kate responded. "For putting her out of her misery and then having someone come out and bury her."

"It's not what you owe me. It's what I owe you. So, tell you what, why don't we just call it even?"

"I don't understand," Katie said.

"Look lady, here's how it is, and I'm gonna say it only once. I've got nothing to prove and neither have you. We did what we did because it was the right thing to do. You conducted yourself with such dignity, you left me in awe. I only hope my kids show half the class you showed that day. You are a very special person who owes nothing to nobody. As for Marty, he's my nephew. He did what he did not for you and not for me, but because it was something that had to be done. Burying that cow gave you full closure, it gave me closure, and it gave Marty something he rarely gets to feel working in the oil patch where everything comes back to money. It gave him a sense of his own humanity, something he told me he'd never felt before. So now let's get those critters loaded shall we, or are we gonna stand here yakkin' all dang day?"

Closure can only come with perspective, and maybe with a new and deeper understanding of one's own mortality. It was only when Katie endeavored to articulate her thoughts on paper that she realized it was not so much what one single cow had done for her and had meant to her, but how utterly inadequate words were in expressing the absolutes of life. Before she had been launched on her country journey, she knew only the realities of urban cookie cutter life; a life where sameness and conformity and image were paramount. Then she had been thrown literally into another set of dimensions. Her life before the farm had been flat-screen TV. The farm had transformed it into live improvised theatre, complete with all of the props. She had not so much learned independence as come to live it, not so much sought understanding but immersed herself in it. These were things that could never be unlearned or taken from her. They had become a part of her identity, an integral part of who she was. It was this that Stewart had been alluding to, the unequivocal dignity garnered by being who you are, and who you are destined to be, without losing sleep as to how others might perceive you.

And so she wrote…

"Lucky, oh Lucky, you were just a cow, and I could always have seen you as just a cow. Yet you were so much more, ah yes, so much more: a phenomenon, a presence, influential so far beyond the merely bovine. You were a part of me, so much a part of me that when you died, a part of me died with you. But then again, you died because we so decided, you and I together, and so we shall always be bound inextricably together. So, for all that you did for me, for all that you made me, I thank you and I love you."

Author Biography

Colin and Felicity Manuel have farmed near Rocky Mountain House, Alberta, since 1983. Both were born and raised on farms in East Africa; farming in Canada, therefore, brought a whole new perspective to working the land. As with any newcomers to a country, they became keenly aware of the very notion of "perspective", particularly in terms of how they saw things and how they themselves were seen. This got the author thinking … How might a cow see things, particularly a cow with a keen sense of humour? How might such a cow view man himself? The rest, as they say, is in the story!

Illustrator Biography

   Shirley Jackson lives in the Battle Lake area of Alberta where she has farmed with her husband Steve since 1980. Like the author and his wife, they raise purebred Blonde D'Aquitaine cattle. As the illustrations clearly show, Shirley has a deep appreciation for the humour one encounters every farming day, and that is what makes her artwork so special! If you have never given any consideration to whether a cow can express happiness, romance, or anger, take a good look at the pictures. Enjoy! And a great big thank you to both Shirley and Steve, her humorous sidekick!